PICTURES
IN THE DARK

IAN STUART

PUBLISHED FOR THE CRIME CLUB BY

DOUBLEDAY & COMPANY, INC.

GARDEN CITY, NEW YORK

1986

All of the characters in this book
are fictitious, and any resemblance
to actual persons, living or dead,
is purely coincidental.

Library of Congress Cataloging-in-Publication Data
Stuart, Ian.
Pictures in the dark.
I. Title.
PR6069.T77P5   1986   823'.914   85-25280
ISBN 0-385-23500-3

For Indira
who helped so much

PICTURES
IN THE DARK

ONE

The plane flew straight into the wood. Its wings, striking the trees, were torn, crumpled, from the fuselage. The nose hit another tree and disintegrated in a mass of twisted metal.

After the first tearing impact the silence was almost eerie. Then petrol, dripping from a fractured pipe onto the engine, ignited. Flames licked up inside the shattered cockpit and within seconds the plane was an inferno.

It had been another hot day, but with evening the heat had mellowed. In front of me the twenty-acre field stretched away towards the hedge that marked the boundary of my farm. Beyond it, lost in the dusk now, Bridgeman's land sloped up to the little wood half a mile away. The wheat rustled softly. Given reasonable luck, in another two or three weeks it would be ready for combining.

I felt an easy contentment. There was still time for storms to ruin everything, but for the present the crops looked well. I wished Pat could have been here to see them; she would have shared my pleasure. But already it was too long for the moment's regret to last or to go very deep. Time was healing even that wound.

I turned, called, "Brandy!" and started to walk back towards the house. The labrador bounded over and followed at my heels, panting.

I was halfway across the meadow when I heard the plane.

The sound came from behind me, seeming so low I turned again to look, but there were no lights. Noises were deceptive at night; the plane was probably farther away than I had thought. Either that or it was so low its lights were hidden by the ridge. Dangerously low. I glanced at my watch: ten minutes past nine.

Quite a lot of aircraft flew over the farm, big jets from Luton, R.A.F. machines and light planes from the small airfields in the district. This sounded like one of the last. If so, it was late for it to be up; in another quarter of an hour it would be dark.

The bullocks in the meadow were shifting and snuffling. I unhooked the gate that led into the yard and Brandy nosed through. Then I heard the crash and stopped, the hook still in my hand.

There was no explosion but the noise was still loud enough to be startling after the silence. All I could see was the long low line of the hedge on the other side of the meadow; everything else was lost in darkness. And I couldn't hear the plane any more.

I started to run back across the meadow. Beyond, in the field, the wheat dragged at my legs, slowing me and sapping my energy. I ploughed through it. Brandy had apparently decided this was a game. He bounded ahead of me, his broad, muscular back appearing every second or two above the corn. Once I twisted an ankle and swore.

I was halfway across the field when the plane's petrol tanks exploded. There was a sudden shocking eruption of flame, vivid against the darkening sky, followed almost at once by a roar of sound. It seemed to roll down the slope in waves, engulfing me. Brandy stopped in his tracks, whimpering.

There was no gap in the hedge that separated my land from Bridgeman's but near one corner of the field it grew more thinly and I headed that way, thankful for what light remained. The patch of sparser growth extended only a few feet and it took me several seconds to locate it. When I did, strong new shoots whipped my face, stinging it, but I forced my way through.

Fortunately Bridgeman's field was pasture and in spite of the slope I could run faster here than through the wheat. Ahead, the wood was silhouetted against the flames. Sparks showered upward into the darkness. Away to the left I could see lights on in the house and what looked like a car's headlamps shining this way.

The plane had crashed into the far side of the wood and the flames were leaping up through the branches. When I reached it I could see the rear end of the fuselage and the tail plane projecting from the trees; the rest was a burning mass.

Two men were already there, their faces lit by the flames. I recognised Bridgeman and his manager, Foskett. Bridgeman saw me coming and turned. He was about fifty, a heavily built man with dark, thinning hair and a pallid complexion. He wasn't a farmer; he had some sort of business in London, and Foskett ran the place. They had been here six or seven months and I had only seen Bridgeman two or three times and then never to speak to. Foskett I had met occasionally. He was taller than his boss and rangy with a long nose, and hair that grew down over his forehead. I disliked him. He was a poor farmer and according to gossip in the village he was swindling Bridgeman. It was probably true.

"Keep away!" Bridgeman shouted. He looked angry but I supposed it was only shock; he could hardly object to my being on his land in the circumstances.

I stood where I was, regaining my breath. Beside me Brandy whimpered again and shied away from the heat.

"Did the pilot get out?" I asked when I could speak.

"I don't know," Bridgeman replied. "We were too late. It was an inferno; we couldn't get near."

"There's nothing anyone can do," Foskett said brusquely.

If he suspected I was going to show them up by trying, he needn't have worried—it was only too obviously hopeless.

A girl in jeans came running up from the direction of the house. I hadn't seen her before and supposed she was Bridgeman's daughter Stephanie. She was said to be an actress and spent most of the time in London, a slim, lovely girl of about nineteen with long blond hair.

"Ricky!" she cried. Her voice rose on a desperate note and she sounded close to tears. "Why aren't you doing something?"

"It's not Ricky," Bridgeman told her curtly. "Go back to the house. There's nothing anybody can do."

She stared at him, her eyes wide with shock or horror or something else I couldn't put a name to. "But—" she began.

"I said, go back to the house," her father told her harshly.

I didn't blame him; it was no place for a girl. Nor for a man, for that matter.

She stood there staring at him for another moment, then turned and walked away, shoulders slumped. I heard her catch her breath in a sob as she passed me. I was going to ask Bridgeman if the pilot was somebody they knew but he had walked away to where Foskett was standing.

The flames had reached the tail now and there was a good deal of dense black smoke. I inhaled some of it and choked. The heat scorched my face and arms and I moved farther away, towards the other men.

"Have you called the fire service?" I asked.

"Yes," Bridgeman said.

They should be here soon, I thought. Not that they would be able to do anything except prevent the fire from destroying the whole wood. Already two or three of the trees nearest the plane were well alight.

The tail section was only a few feet above the ground; the plane must have ploughed straight into the wood, not crashed on it from above. That meant it had been flying far too low and explained why I hadn't seen any lights. Maybe the pilot had been in trouble and was looking for somewhere to land. Poor devil. The chances of his getting out before the crash must have been almost nil but at least he wouldn't have known much about it.

"There's nothing we can do," Bridgeman said, almost repeating Foskett's words. He made it sound less pointed but he didn't move and I guessed he meant I might as well go. He was right—standing staring at the blazing wreckage was too ghoulish for my taste and I didn't want to see what was in the plane when the fire was put out.

"No," I agreed. "I'll get back. Good night."

"Good night," Bridgeman said.

Foskett didn't say anything.

I started walking back down the slope. In the light of the fire I could see scraps of debris littering the turf, most of it badly charred. Then something that glittered dully in the yellow light caught my eye and I stooped to pick it up. It was a small silver box. I looked over my shoulder; Bridgeman and Foskett were hidden by the corner of the wood.

The box must have been blown here by the force of the blast when the petrol tanks exploded. In which case it belonged to the pilot. Or his estate. I was too tired and too lethargic to walk back just to hand it over to Bridgeman. Especially after he had made it so clear I'd better go. Anyway, it wasn't his and I could give it to the police as well as he could. I slipped it into my pocket and walked on. Brandy, subdued now, padded along beside me, his tongue hanging out.

"Good boy," I said.

He looked up at me, panting, and wagged his tail.

This time I pushed through the hedge more cautiously, holding back the whippy twigs. And I didn't plough through the wheat, I walked round the edge of the field. All that remained of the sunset was a single orange streak low in the sky.

When I reached the meadow I looked back. The fire was still burning but the flames were lower now and I wondered if the fire brigade had arrived.

Letting myself in by the back door, I kicked off my shoes and padded along to the big room at the front of the house I used as a living-room. When Pat was alive it was our dining-room but now I was on my own I had no use for more than one room. Soon after she died I had brought two of the big old chairs in here and I hardly ever went into the drawing-room now.

The house had been built about 1840. It had no architectural pretensions but it was well proportioned and the rooms were large and airy. The furniture, bits and pieces we had bought when we were married or acquired from our parents plus one or two things we had seen and liked, was solid and comfortable. I poured myself a stiff Scotch, added a little water and sank into one of the easy chairs. I was tired; I had been up since six and worked pretty hard all day. But I knew that wasn't the reason. I was used to work; it was reaction.

Something pressed against my thigh. I had forgotten the little box; now I took it out and examined it. It was about two and a half inches long and an inch deep, the top elaborately decorated with a raised representation of a castle. There was a small dent in one end but it was clean, it couldn't have been lying where I found it very long. I knew next to nothing about silver but it looked to me like a snuff box. I turned it over. There were hallmarks on the bottom: a lion, an anchor, a head, the initials "NM" and a small letter "m". I knew the lion was the assay mark and I thought I remembered hearing somewhere that an anchor signified that an object had been made in Birmingham, but I had no idea what the other marks meant except that one of them was the date and another the maker's.

I opened the lid. The tiny hinges were beautifully made and the lid fitted perfectly with the hallmarks repeated on the inside. The box was empty. I closed it again and put it away in a drawer of the sideboard. I had to go into Stallford tomorrow. I would take it to the police then; they would know what to do with it.

I finished my whisky, locked up and went to bed.

As it turned out I didn't have to go to the police, they came to me. I was up in one of the top fields helping Fred Gainsford, my stockman, when I saw a car with a Police sign on its roof coming along the track from the lane. It stopped by the house and two men got out. Leaving Fred to carry on, I went to meet them.

They were both in uniform, a sergeant and a constable. I knew the village sergeant; these were strangers.

"Mr. Fordham?" the sergeant enquired.

"Yes."

"We understand you saw the plane that crashed last night, sir."

I supposed Bridgeman must have told them. Or Foskett.

"Only after it came down," I said. "There wasn't much of it left by the time I got there."

"No." He was a pleasant, intelligent-looking man of about forty. The constable was younger and stayed by the car. "You didn't see it before it crashed, then?"

I shook my head. "I only heard it—it was almost dark. It sounded as if it was flying very low. Then I heard the crash and ran over to see if there was anything I could do."

"You didn't hear the engine cut out before the crash, sir? As if the pilot was in trouble?"

"No."

"And it was on fire when you got to it?"

"Yes. It exploded when I was halfway there." I hesitated. "The pilot was killed, I suppose?"

"I'm afraid so, sir."

"Was he from round here?"

"We don't think so. The plane belonged to a flying club in Berkshire."

That meant they hadn't identified him yet. I wasn't surprised; there couldn't have been much left to identify by the time the fire was put out. Either that or for some reason of their own they weren't saying.

"Who was there when you arrived, sir?" the sergeant asked.

"Mr. Bridgeman and Foskett, his manager. Miss Bridgeman came but her father sent her back."

The sergeant nodded. "Well, I don't think there's anything else. Good morning, sir."

" 'Morning," I said.

I watched them climb back into their car, reverse and drive off along the track. They had almost reached the lane before I remembered the snuffbox and then it was too late to call them back. It didn't matter—I would take it when I went into Stallford. I went to rejoin Fred.

When I returned to the house an hour later Tom Carr was bending over one of the tractors, tinkering with the engine. He looked up when he heard me coming and wiped an oily hand across his forehead.

"Bloody thing's broken down again," he reported morosely.

Tom was twenty-two, a lanky fellow with a cheeky grin. With Fred Gainsford he comprised my entire labour force. Years ago my father had employed ten men on his two farms and as many again had come in the evenings at harvest time. There had been horses then and binders instead of combines. Mechanisation was almost a dirty word. Times had changed on farms more than most places.

"What's wrong with it this time?" I enquired. Usually Tom was a cheery character; now he looked fed up.

Of my three tractors this was the oldest. It was hopelessly unreliable and I should have got rid of it months ago but I clung to it as if, by doing so, however often it let me down, I was ensuring that I got value for the money it had cost me secondhand three years ago. Pat had always maintained I was stubborn; maybe she had been right.

"Don't know," Tom replied, bending over it again.

There was no breeze in the yard and it was hotter than ever.

"I'll be with you in a few minutes," I told him.

I went into the kitchen. Too hot for coffee. I opened a can of beer and cut myself a thick slice of new bread and a hunk of real Cheddar. Heat rarely affected my appetite.

When I had eaten the bread and cheese and drunk the beer I went back to the yard. Tom and I worked on the tractor for the next hour. By the time we finished, it was running again and it was too late to go into Stallford. I told myself it didn't matter, tomorrow would do. I couldn't spare the time this afternoon.

TWO

I finished work just after six. When I rounded the corner of the end barn there was a car parked in front of the house, a low, powerful-looking Jaguar XJS with gleaming bodywork. None of my friends owned anything so impressive—mostly their cars were Fords or Vauxhalls—and I wondered who my visitor was.

As I walked over a girl climbed out of the driving seat. I stared. Her skin was dark and she was wearing a sari that fell in graceful folds of green and white round her slim figure. She saw me coming and waited.

"Good evening," I said.

"Good evening. Can you tell me how to get to Langley Farm?" Her voice was deep, the accent upper-class English with hardly a trace of accent.

That explained the car, I thought. The Bridgemans' friends would own Jaguars. Or Rolls. Bridgeman had a Silver Shadow.

"It's over there," I told her, pointing to the low ridge. "The house is to the left of that wood."

"Oh."

She stood looking across the fields as if the scene fascinated her.

"You'll have to go down the lane to the main road," I said. "Turn left there and it's the first on the left. There's a long drive."

"Thank you."

Still she didn't move. I had a strange idea that although she had asked me where it was she wasn't keen to go there.

"You know the Bridgemans?" I asked her.

"Is that their name? No, I've never met them." She turned and looked at me. She had high cheekbones and large, beautiful eyes. It was a proud, reserved face. "What are they like?"

"I hardly know them. They haven't been there long."

She hesitated. "Did you see the plane that crashed last night?"

It was a natural enough question if she had heard about it but for some reason it startled me. I had a feeling she had had to almost force herself to ask. Yet she hadn't sounded distressed. Not sufficiently, anyway, for the pilot to have been close to her.

I nodded. "Yes."

"You weren't there?"

"I went. There wasn't anything I could do." Something made me ask, "Did you know him?"

The moment the words were out I regretted them. It was no business of mine and if the pilot had been a friend she would think I was prying.

"He was my cousin," she said. Her eyes were strangely expressionless.

"I'm sorry."

"Thank you."

Suddenly I remembered the snuffbox. I might as well give it to her; she would know what to do with it and it would save me taking it to the police.

"I found something," I told her. "If you'll come into the house I'll get it."

"What is it?"

"A little silver box. I was going to take it to the police tomorrow."

She frowned, then nodded. "Thank you, I'll take it."

She tossed back the end of her sari with a graceful movement of her arm and we walked across to the house.

"I'm sorry, we'll have to go in this way," I told her.

I opened the back door and took her through to the living room. It was a mess. Clutter may give a house a lived-in appearance but it doesn't necessarily make it look better. I hadn't bothered to clear away the remains of my lunch and there was still an empty beer can on the table beside the dirty plates and that morning's paper. The sunlight streaming in at the window didn't help. She stood there taking it in.

"Sorry about the mess," I said. "I'm on my own."

She made no comment. I saw her looking at the photograph of Pat on the sideboard. She would probably think my wife was away for a few days and I was pigging it until she returned.

The snuffbox was in the top drawer, I took it out and handed it to her. She held it in her hand studying it. Then she turned it over.

"Where did you find this?" she asked.

"In the field when I was coming home. I'm afraid it's dented." Just in time I stopped myself saying it must have been blown there by the explosion. "It was his, wasn't it?"

"Yes, I'm sure it was." She smiled briefly. "Thank you for looking after it, Mr.—"

"Fordham. Clive Fordham."

"I am Rekha Graham."

It was a pretty name. It suited her, I thought. She was holding the box in her left hand and I saw she was wearing a wide gold wedding ring.

"It looks valuable," I remarked.

"Yes." She was still studying the little box.

I walked across to open the door for her.

"Thank you for this and for telling me the way, Mr. Fordham," she said.

I watched her walk over to the Jaguar and slide into the driving seat. The door closed with a soft thud. It was a strange world, I reflected: a lovely Indian girl in a sari driving a car like that coming here. Kipling had been wrong. I watched her drive down the track to the lane, pause there and turn left; then I walked back to the house.

I was getting my supper when I decided to make a note of the hallmarks on the snuffbox before I forgot them. I don't know what made me do it; possibly it was only curiosity. I rarely handled anything of value apart from the stock on the farm. I found a writing pad and jotted them down.

When I had eaten my meal I carried the dirty things out to the kitchen and washed up, then settled down to read the paper for half an hour. I had thought of playing tennis that evening but it was too late now and, anyway, the inclination had gone. I watched a couple of hours' television and went to bed early.

The last thing I remember thinking about before I fell asleep was Rekha Graham's expression as she stood looking across the valley to the wood where her cousin's plane had crashed. They couldn't have been very close; she hadn't shown any sign of distress all the time she was here. And she hadn't spoken as if she had seen the snuffbox before. All the same, most people would have been upset. A hard young woman, I thought, for all her charm. I found myself disliking her.

So why did I want to see her again?

The next day was Thursday. When I woke it was raining, a persistent soaking drizzle. It must have started during the night—moisture was dripping off the trees beside the house and there were puddles on the track. I cursed, but provided it didn't last too long and the wind didn't get up it wouldn't do any harm.

All the same, I spent two or three hours mooching about without doing anything very useful, listening to Fred and Tom grumbling. Then I got out my old Cortina Estate and drove in to Stallford to the bank.

George Challess was there. Our fathers had been friends and we had been at school together. Now he owned the farm adjoining mine on the other side from Bridgeman's. He waited while I cashed my cheque and then we went across to the Red Lion together.

It was a pleasant pub and meeting there on Thursday mornings had become something of a ritual. There were several other farmers already there, mostly men about my own age. Somebody said something about the crash and they seemed to think I would know all about it. One had heard that the plane had come from Denham and the pilot was a well-known actor, another that it was an R.A.F. machine testing secret equipment.

I told them what I knew. For some reason I didn't say anything about Rekha Graham's visit, but thinking about it reminded me of the snuffbox. The piece of paper on which I had scribbled down the hallmarks was in my wallet. I finished my beer, said goodbye to the others and walked out into the street.

When I was a kid there weren't many antique shops in small country towns; now they blossomed everywhere. There were two in Stallford, the better of them owned by a man named Harvey. At least I supposed it was the better— it was smarter and to my inexpert eye the silver and jewellery in one window and furniture in the other looked good. Judged by the prices on the labels, they should have been. I decided to try there first.

I had never been in an antique shop in my life. The few

good pieces Pat and I bought we had picked up at sales and I was a little embarrassed at asking for information when I had no intention of buying anything. Especially as I had no valid excuse for wanting it.

Harvey came through from the back of the shop when I walked in. He was a dapper, rather florid man and he was wearing a smart suit and a bow tie. I was in the clothes I wore round the farm and my embarrassment increased. He was probably hoping I wouldn't leave too much muck on his floor.

"I wonder if you could give me some information," I explained, taking out my wallet and extracting the slip of paper. "A friend of mine has a little silver box with these hallmarks and she's trying to find out anything she can about it. She thinks it's a snuffbox."

I was relieved that he didn't look down his nose. Nor did he suggest I should try the public library. In fact, he appeared to be interested.

"What is it like?" he asked.

"It's about two and a half inches long and an inch deep and there's a castle on the top," I told him. "The anchor's the mark for Birmingham, isn't it?"

"Yes." If he was surprised I knew even so little he was too well mannered to show it. "The lion is the assay mark and the head is George the Third's. The 'NM' means it was made by Nathaniel Mills. The 'm' is the date mark—1810, I think. Let me just check that."

He disappeared into the back of the shop and reappeared a minute later holding a small grey-covered book. I saw the title *Bradbury's Book of Hallmarks*.

"I get a bit confused with date marks," he confessed, turning the pages. "Yes, I was right, 1810. Are the hallmarks on the lid as well as the bottom?"

"Yes."

"Is there a shield on the base?"

"Yes."

"If not it's a pretty safe bet the design on top was added later. I don't know whether your friend knows, but Mills was one of the best makers. If the box is in good condition it could be worth five or six hundred pounds."

I nearly whistled. I had guessed it might be fairly valuable but not that it could be worth so much. I wondered if Rekha Graham would know and what she intended doing with it. Had her cousin left a widow? If so, presumably now it would be hers.

"Is your friend thinking of selling it?" Harvey asked.

"I don't know," I admitted.

"If she is, I would advise her to take it to one of the big London firms to have it properly valued."

"Thank you, I'll tell her," I said. I had an uneasy feeling that what I was doing was slightly underhand.

"It's a pleasure."

He came to the door with me and said, "Goodbye." It was still raining. Amongst the jewellery in the window there was a delicate old brooch, stones I took to be garnets set in gold. Pat would have liked it, I thought. It would have been her birthday next week.

Turning up my collar, I walked back to where I had left my car.

THREE

The inquest was held at Stallford the next day. Even at the time I couldn't have explained why I went—the weather had changed again overnight, it was a fine sunny morning and there was plenty of work to be done on the farm. I told myself it wasn't just morbid curiosity; like it or not, I was involved. Not so much because I had gone to see if I could help as because of the snuffbox and Rekha Graham's visit. And I wanted to see her again.

I still didn't know why she had gone to Langley Farm that evening. Had she wanted to see the place where her cousin died or was there something else? Her manner had been reserved, almost as if she were hiding something, but there was nothing surprising in that—I was a stranger. I wondered what had happened when she went to see the Bridgemans. No doubt they had been sympathetic; what more could they do?

The little courtroom in the town hall had space for only a few members of the public. The crash had aroused a good deal of speculation and it was almost full when I arrived. Watson, the coroner, was an elderly solicitor with a reputation for using his office to make pungent and sometimes damaging comments. In spite of his austere appearance he liked the limelight and today he would be in his element.

I saw Mrs. Graham at once, a conspicuous figure in her sari with her dark beauty. Today the sari was dark, presumably in deference to the occasion. There was an Indian with her but his back was to me and I couldn't see his face.

Bridgeman came in accompanied by a fat, prosperous-looking man with a large nose and heavy horn-rimmed glasses. He was wearing a dark suit and looked like a solicitor.

There was no jury. The coroner explained that he was there to establish the identity of the deceased and the cause of death. Then he called Mrs. Rekha Graham. Apparently if there was a widow she hadn't come.

Mrs. Graham walked forward and murmured something to the officer by the witness box. I couldn't hear what she said but she must have explained that she wasn't a Christian so couldn't take the oath, because old Watson told her that in that case she must affirm. He said it testily, as if he suspected her of deliberately being difficult.

She agreed that her name was Rekha Graham and she lived at 20 Corhampton Court, Hampstead. She had been shown certain personal effects found in the wreckage of the plane including a watch and a ring and had identified them as belonging to her husband, Derek Francis Graham.

I stared at her, startled. That possibility hadn't occurred to me. Why had she said she was his cousin?

She spoke quietly, without any visible sign of emotion. I saw the coroner watching her appraisingly and guessed he was wondering how much allowance he should make for her bereavement.

"When did you last see your husband, Mrs. Graham?" he asked.

"Just over a year ago. We separated then."

Did that explain it? Partly, perhaps.

The last she had heard of him, her husband was working as some sort of agent. He was an experienced pilot and as far as she knew his health was good and he had no financial worries. She had no idea why he should have been flying over Langley Farm that evening.

After a few more routine questions the coroner let her go. She was followed by a police sergeant who had gone to the farm as a result of Bridgeman's 999 call and the fire officer who testified that the station had been alerted at 9:35. When they arrived, the plane was already almost completely destroyed and all his men could do was prevent the fire from spreading.

Bridgeman was the next witness. He had been talking to Foskett when they heard the plane flying very low, then crashing. They had run to the scene but by the time they reached it the fire was burning too fiercely for them to do anything. He thought the crash had occurred at a quarter past nine or a few minutes later.

He was mistaken about that, I thought. My watch had said ten past and it was right to within a minute or so.

A doctor testified that the deceased had died as a result of multiple injuries consistent with the crash and that death must have been instantaneous. I didn't understand the medical technicalities but I was glad Graham had died before the fire started.

Then the coroner called the manager of a flying club in Berkshire who stated that the plane, a Cherokee 140, had belonged to the club and been in good order. Graham had taken off just after 5:30 saying he was flying to Denham but he hadn't landed there. As far as the manager knew, there was no reason why he should have been anywhere near Langley Farm, which was twenty miles farther north. Graham was a fully qualified pilot and a good navigator.

The last witness was a civil aviation inspector who testified that he was not yet in a position to give any opinion as to the cause of the crash. Watson expressed his sympathy to

the widow and adjourned the proceedings and we filed out
into the street, blinking a little in the sunlight.

People began drifting away. I saw Bridgeman and the fat
man walk off towards the car park and looked round for
Mrs. Graham. She came out with the Indian. I saw her
glance in my direction and our eyes met but although we
were no more than a dozen yards apart, she gave no sign of
recognition. Then she said something to her companion
and they followed Bridgeman.

I felt mildly irritated. She had deliberately deceived me
when she came to the farm; now she might at least have had
the courtesy to say "Good morning."

I waited a few minutes in order that we shouldn't meet in
the car park, then retrieved my car and drove home.

Something was puzzling me. The plane had crashed at
ten past nine. I had arrived on the scene only a few minutes
later and when I asked Bridgeman if he had called the fire
service he said he had. Yet the station hadn't received the
call until nine-thirty-five. Emergency calls were delayed occasionally, I knew, but only very rarely and it was unlikely
the local exchange was so busy that evening they hadn't
passed this one on immediately. Had Bridgeman lied and
not made it until he returned to his house? If he hadn't
already rung, the obvious thing would have been for him to
do so when I reminded him. Or send Foskett. Why lie about
it?

Unless he knew more about the plane than he was prepared to admit.

There was something else. When she came running up,
Stephanie had cried out, "Ricky!" Her father had told her it
wasn't Ricky and sent her away. At the time I assumed it was
because the blazing plane was no sight for a girl, but had
there been another reason? And how had he known the
pilot wasn't Ricky?

Stephanie was distraught because she thought she knew him. That suggested they had been expecting a plane to land. But if so, why had Bridgeman waited twenty minutes to call the fire service?

And, after all, Graham's name wasn't Ricky, it was Derek.

It would have taken him not much more than half an hour to fly from the airfield where he had hired the plane to Denham. That left three hours unaccounted for. I didn't know much about flying but I had an idea that even light aircraft were pretty strictly controlled—you couldn't just take off and fly about the sky as the fancy took you. Not unless you were anxious that nobody should know where you were going. And Graham hadn't landed at Denham.

I told myself it was no concern of mine, but I couldn't rid myself of an uneasy feeling that I was involved—and to a greater extent than I had believed.

The lane that led to the village rose fairly steeply for a couple of hundred yards, then dropped before climbing again. Just before the top of the second rise I turned right onto the track that led to my house. I don't think I would have been surprised to see Rekha Graham's XJS parked there. Perhaps I hoped it would be. But the space in front of the house was bare. I left the Ford outside the barn I used as a garage and went to find Tom.

The suspicion that something was wrong haunted me all that afternoon. I could hardly ask Bridgeman if he had lied about ringing the fire service and, if so, why. Nor whether he had known the dead man. And I couldn't approach his daughter or Foskett. That left only one person, if I was going to do anything. Mrs. Graham.

I hadn't consciously tried to memorise the address she gave at the inquest and I don't know why I remembered it now. Perhaps subconsciously I had wanted to remember it.

I toyed with the idea of ringing her to ask if I could come but rejected it; she would probably refuse and I was in no position to insist. Besides, while the telephone has its uses, I usually remember something else I had wanted to say as soon as I have put it down.

There was only one snag about my going to see her: she lived thirty miles from the farm. That meant a wasted journey of twice as far if she wasn't at home or wouldn't see me. Nevertheless I decided to risk it. I knew I wouldn't be satisfied until I had tried to find answers to the questions that were bothering me.

Corhampton Court was pretty obviously a block of flats and Hampstead covered a big area. Half expecting a frosty response, I rang the police there and asked if they could tell me how to find it. They could and did. I thanked them and replaced the receiver with the feeling that at least I was doing something. Exactly what, I had no idea.

Perhaps it was as well I didn't know; if I had known I might have stopped there and then.

I reckoned the best time to arrive would be about six-thirty. If Mrs. Graham had a job and had gone to work that afternoon, she would be home by then and I would catch her before she went out for the evening or had visitors. From what I had seen of her I couldn't imagine her sitting at home grieving. I didn't expect her to be pleased to see me, but that was the least of my worries.

Tom and Fred finished work for the day and left, Tom on the secondhand Honda 125 he had bought last week and on which he lavished as much affection as he did on his pretty girl-friend. I went indoors, had a quick shower, changed and within twenty-five minutes was on my way.

As usual at that time on a Friday afternoon there was a good deal of traffic, and it was even heavier after I joined the M1. Fortunately a lot of it was going north, and there were no real delays until I reached Hendon. Then I drove straight into a jam that stretched for the best part of a mile. I sat there inching forward a few feet at a time, trying to curb my impatience. Already it was twenty past six and I still had to find the road. I told myself that a couple of hours ago I had had no thought of seeing Rekha Graham again and it was ridiculous to be fretting because I would be a few minutes later than I had planned. It didn't help.

At last I was clear of the bottle-neck. I pressed my foot on the accelerator and hoped devoutly that after all this she would be at home.

Corhampton Court turned out to be a large pre-war block in a quiet road near the Heath. The road was blessedly free of yellow lines. I parked, locked the car and walked across the semi-circle of asphalt.

Number 20 was on the first floor. I rang the doorbell and waited. There was no answer and I was about to ring again when Mrs. Graham opened the door.

She eyed me as if she had never seen me before. The dark sari she had worn at the inquest had gone and she was wearing the one she had worn when she came to the farm.

"Good evening," she said. Her deep, rich voice held a faint note of enquiry.

"Good evening, Mrs. Graham. I'm Clive Fordham."

"Yes, I remember."

"I wonder if you could spare me a few minutes?"

She hesitated. "Very well. Come in." Her tone was hardly friendly but it wasn't openly hostile either. That was something, I supposed. More than I had expected.

I followed her across a small hall and into a big room with a dining area at one end. A window took up a good deal of one wall; the others were hung with pictures, mostly landscapes and drawings of Indian scenes, though there was one still life. They were originals and I wondered if she had acquired the landscapes with the flat—they didn't fit my image of her.

When she turned, her expression revealed nothing but I had a sudden impression that she was on the defensive.

"Why have you come?" she demanded.

I hesitated. On the way there I had tried to think of some excuse, without coming up with anything that sounded plausible. I could tell her the truth, that there were things about the crash I couldn't understand, but she would say it was no business of mine and tell me to go. I couldn't blame her; it wasn't.

"Why did you tell me you were Graham's cousin?" I asked.

It was her turn not to answer immediately. Then she said, "I thought it would save me having to answer a lot of questions. And I didn't want sympathy."

Touché, I thought. But she was talking about this morning, not now.

"Were they the only reasons?"

"Yes. I really can't see it mattered."

"No," I agreed. After all, why had her lying annoyed me so? "Your husband knew the Bridgemans, didn't he?"

Her eyes were blank. "Mr. Fordham, why have you come here to question me like this?" she asked coldly.

"If you'll answer, I'll try to explain."

She shrugged. "It's no use asking me about Derek. I don't know."

"He could have known them?"

"Oh yes, he could. He knew a lot of people I didn't. Anyway, I hadn't seen him for over a year."

"I know. I heard you say so at the inquest."

"There you are, then."

It sounded like a dismissal. I ignored it and after a moment she reminded me, "You said you'd explain why you came. We'd better sit down."

Hardly gracious, I thought. She sat at one end of a big settee. I took a chair facing her. Her face was expressionless as a mask and I remembered how she had looked that evening staring across at the wood. Again I had an impression of vulnerability that disturbed and intrigued me.

"Why didn't you speak when you saw me outside the town hall this morning?" I asked.

"People who ask questions like that usually get answers they don't like," she observed tartly.

"The people I know are polite enough to say 'Good morning' even to those they don't like," I retorted.

She looked surprised. "Yes, I'm sorry. It was just—I couldn't face any more of it."

Deliberately or not, she had succeeded in putting me in the wrong.

"I didn't intend asking you anything," I told her.

"I've said I'm sorry." She seemed more relaxed now but there was still something guarded in her manner. "Why *are* you here, Mr. Fordham?"

"Did his friends call your husband Ricky?" I asked.

This time there was no mistaking her surprise. She didn't look pleased, either.

"Some of them did," she agreed.

It had been a shot in the dark and I felt absurdly pleased with myself.

"His plane crashed about ten past nine," I said. "It took me five or six minutes to get there. As soon as I did I asked Bridgeman if he had called the fire people and he said he had."

She frowned. "What about it?"

"At the inquest the fire officer said they didn't get the call until nine thirty-five."

"Calls are delayed sometimes."

"A nine-nine-nine call in a rural area at that time?"

"Are you suggesting something?"

"No, not really. It just looks as if Bridgeman lied to me about having called them and I wonder why."

"I've no idea."

Was that the truth? If it was, still she might suspect something.

"It wouldn't have made any difference if they had got there straightaway. They couldn't have done anything," she said.

"No," I agreed. "Why was your husband flying so low when it was almost dark? His engine didn't cut out—I heard it right up to the moment he crashed. And why did he say he was going to Denham? It wouldn't have taken him more than half an hour or so to fly there."

"You sound like a policeman." Somehow her scorn didn't ring true.

"I'm just curious," I told her. "I wonder why people have lied when there didn't seem any reason for it."

I hadn't meant her, but she took it that way. "I said I didn't want to answer a lot of questions."

"And Bridgeman?"

"I've no idea." She paused. The window was open and I could hear the steady hum of traffic on the main road a hundred yards away. "How did you know Derek liked people to call him Ricky?"

I had been wondering when she would get round to that.

"Have you met Bridgeman's daughter?" I asked her.

She shook her head. If her husband had meant so little to her she wouldn't be hurt by what I was going to say, I thought.

"She's about twenty. Very pretty. I believe she's an actress. Just after I got to the wood she came running up. She cried out, 'Ricky!' Her father told her it wasn't Ricky and to go back to the house."

A shadow passed briefly over the dark, beautiful features.

"He thought it was more—trendy than Derek. More sexy."

I wondered if she had left him because of other women. For some reason it didn't occur to me that he might have left her.

"There's something else," I said.

"Oh?"

"The snuffbox I found. It was made by Nathaniel Mills in 1810 and it's valuable."

For the first time I saw a spark of amusement in her eyes. "Are you an expert on old silver, Mr. Fordham?"

"Far from it," I admitted. "There's a good antique dealer in Stallford."

"Vernon Harvey."

"You know him?" I was surprised.

"We've met." She didn't elaborate. "I suppose you think Derek was trying to land at the farm to see the girl?"

"No."

"Oh?" Her eyebrows went up.

"I think he knew her but he was going to see Bridgeman himself."

"Why?"

"I don't know," I confessed, "but from the way Bridgeman's behaved I've an idea it was something he doesn't want people to know about."

"You're probably right," Mrs. Graham said. She toyed with the fringe on the settee. "Derek was a crook."

FOUR

The revelation itself wasn't as shocking as her calm admission of it. I stared at her.

"I'm sorry," she said, "would you like something to drink? You've come a long way, haven't you?" She smiled again but this time it was mischievously, without any apparent malice. "What would you like? Sherry? Whisky? Gin and tonic?"

"Gin and tonic, please," I said. I would have preferred beer but at least gin and tonic would be cool.

"Or beer?" she suggested, standing up.

"Beer then, please."

She went out of the room, leaving the door ajar. I heard a door open, then close again with a soft thud. A refrigerator. She returned carrying a can of pale ale and a glass of what looked like white wine. Crossing to the sideboard, she took out a pewter tankard and poured the beer into it. She did it properly, letting the beer flow down the side. As if she were used to doing it. I wondered if she kept a few cans for her men friends when they came here. One man, perhaps. Maybe she didn't live alone, although there was no sign of a man's being there—no slippers or men's magazines, no pipe on the mantelpiece.

"Cheers," she said.

"Cheers."

The beer was colder than I really liked but I drank it

gratefully, surprised how thirsty I was. The atmosphere in
the room had changed and I felt relaxed.

"You're shocked, aren't you?" she remarked.

"No." It was true, I had begun to suspect that Graham
hadn't been as honest as he might have been.

"You looked shocked."

"Did I? It was the way you said it."

"You think I should have more respect for the dead. *De
mortuis* and all that."

"No."

"I disliked Derek and despised him. He was weak and
greedy and vain. And he was lazy. He had a lot of shady
friends but he wasn't crooked in the way you're thinking—
he wasn't a burglar or a bank robber. He just didn't care if
what he was doing was dishonest as long as he could make
something out of it."

Everyone knew people like that. They drifted along making a living by shady deals. All the same, she wasn't painting
a very attractive picture.

"What did he do?" I asked.

"His job, you mean? I don't know what he'd been doing
lately. Buying and selling anything he could make a profit
from, I expect."

"Silver?"

She regarded me thoughtfully, her eyes blank. "Perhaps."

"Had he been in the antiques business, then?"

I knew I was asking too many questions, far more than I
had any right to ask. But she didn't seem to mind any
longer. Perhaps she was even glad to talk to a stranger
about it.

"He was once," she replied.

"That's how you knew about the hallmarks on the snuffbox."

She laughed, surprised. It was an unexpectedly merry sound. "How persistent you are, Mr. Fordham! No, I didn't learn that from Derek."

I remembered she had met Harvey. Perhaps she was in the business herself. Anyway, it was time I finished my beer and went.

"I'm sorry I've asked so many questions," I apologised, standing up. "I daresay it's no business of mine."

"No." She acknowledged it as a fact, without resentment. "What are you going to do now?"

"Go home." It was my turn to be surprised. Then I realised she had meant what was I going to do about my suspicions? What could I do? I wasn't even sure I wanted to do anything any longer. If anything was wrong it was up to the police.

"Your wife will be expecting you."

I remembered she had seen the photograph of Pat on my sideboard.

"She died three years ago," I said.

I didn't tell her Pat had died on an operating table in Stallford Hospital. The operation was straightforward but the anaesthetist had made a mistake. He was an Indian. It was some time before I got round to admitting to myself that everyone made mistakes. They didn't have to be Indian or American or anything else, just human.

"I'm sorry."

"Yes." I never knew what to say when people sympathised. Like most grief, mine was a personal thing and even sympathy was a sort of intrusion. But at least now I could talk about Pat without that terrible bitter sense of loss. And I had good memories. I was lucky.

Mrs. Graham hesitated as if she were on the point of saying something else. But if she was, she changed her mind. She stood up and came to the door with me.

"Goodbye, Mr. Fordham."

"Goodbye," I said.

We shook hands. Hers was very slim; it felt smooth and tiny in mine.

I turned and started down the stairs. A man was coming up, the slightly built Indian about my own age who had been with Rekha Graham that morning. He eyed me appraisingly as we passed.

Behind me I heard her say, "Ravi!" She sounded pleased.

"Hallo, Rekha."

The door closed behind them then. I went on down the stairs and out to my car.

I had learnt a little but there were still a lot of questions to which I didn't know the answers. For one thing, I had no idea what Graham had been doing between five-thirty and nine-ten and I had a feeling it was important.

I was undressing for bed before the obvious question occurred to me: why was he carrying a snuffbox worth several hundred pounds around with him? His wife had hinted that he had always wanted to impress people, but a snuffbox wasn't like an expensive watch; it wasn't on permanent display and not many people would appreciate its value.

The question was so obvious I wondered why I hadn't thought of it before. Had it occurred to Rekha Graham? Whatever else she might be, I was pretty sure she wasn't slow-witted.

She might know the reason but to me it was just one more unanswered question. It didn't explain why he had flown to see Bridgeman when it was almost dark. Or even if he had. I was convinced he hadn't been going to see Stephanie; if he had been, there would have been no reason for Bridgeman to pretend he didn't know him. Landing on a rough meadow in near darkness suggested a desire for secrecy.

Then I remembered something I had almost forgotten until now. When I ran to the wood I had seen a car's headlights shining towards me from somewhere near the house. And there had been more lights on in the house itself than I would have expected. Had they been switched on to guide Graham in? A sort of improvised flare path?

For the umpteenth time I told myself it was nothing to do with me. Why should I bother when everybody else appeared to be satisfied? I turned off the bedside lamp and settled down.

But my brain was too active for sleep. Questions and ideas chased each other round until they lost all sense and became part of a phantasmagoric pattern, confused and disturbing. Mixed up with them was the memory of Rekha Graham looking at me, her eyes laughing. Had she been laughing at me? She had appeared to be talking frankly, but what had she really told me? Only that her husband had been no good. I suspected she knew more than she had been prepared to admit. Perhaps if there was a mystery about his death she was a part of it.

At last I fell asleep.

I didn't sleep long. When I woke everything was quiet. I rolled over and switched on the light. The clock said five minutes to one. I had expected it to be later.

The curtains were stirring in the draught from the open window. I put on my glasses, turned the light off again and padded across the room to look out. A good deal of cloud had blown up, obscuring the moon, and the yard was in darkness.

I could hear a car coming up the lane from the main road. Then it stopped. A courting couple parking on their way home, I guessed. The air was soft and warm.

I thought of Rekha Graham and her smart flat. It was pleasant enough but I would hate to live in London with all its fumes and traffic.

Thinking about her reminded me of the crash. If I was right, Bridgeman had deliberately delayed calling the fire service because he wanted the plane to be completely destroyed. That must mean he knew there was something on it he daren't risk being found. What?

It couldn't be silver: even that fire wouldn't have destroyed metal. I knew that after any blaze there were nearly always scraps that escaped the flames. And the wreckage hadn't been carted away yet. I had been working on that side of the farm this afternoon and I would have heard if it had been. Perhaps the authorities had insisted it be left.

Sleep was out of the question now. It was a fine night; I would go and have a look. I drew the curtains, pulled on a shirt and an old pair of trousers and rummaged in the bottom of the wardrobe for some tennis shoes.

When I entered the kitchen Brandy looked up, tail thumping the floor.

"Not this time, boy," I told him.

My torch was in a drawer of one of the cabinets. I slipped it into a pocket of my trousers, switched off the light and let myself out of the house.

Outside it was as quiet as it had been indoors. The courting couple must be still at it. I felt a pang of envy and for no reason at all wondered what it would be like to hold Rekha Graham like that. She couldn't be as cold as she tried to appear, not with eyes that sparked with mischief as hers did.

I waited for perhaps half a minute while my eyes adjusted to the darkness, then set off across the yard towards the meadow. The turf was dry underfoot and I walked fast.

The wheat sighed in the twenty-acre field. I kept to the edge, turning left at the bottom towards the thinner part of the hedge. It would have been easier to find it if I had used my torch but some instinct warned me not to. I don't think I had any idea of somebody watching; it was simply that a light would have made me feel exposed.

I still didn't know what I expected to find. Even if I would find anything. I just knew I wouldn't be easy in my mind until I had looked. The fact that I would be trespassing didn't trouble me at all.

After a minute's searching I found the place in the hedge and eased my way through, trying to hold back the twigs that snapped at me. Once on the other side it was easier going up the grassy slope. Away to my left the house was in darkness. I reached the edge of the wood and stopped. By now I was accustomed to the dim light and could see well enough to find my way.

The plane had crashed on the other side. I walked forward cautiously, my plimsolls making no sound, though the chances of anyone hearing me anyway were remote. When I reached the far corner I stopped. The wreckage should be twenty yards or so to my right. I started in that direction. Then, somewhere in the trees almost directly above me, an owl hooted and I started. The odd, familiar sound had seemed unnaturally loud in the silence. For a moment I stood stock still, my nerves tense, straining for any other noise. There was nothing and I edged forward again.

I could see the plane now. Or what was left of it; there wasn't much. Only the tail plane and fin projecting from a tangled, charred mess of metal a few feet above the ground. It was darker than ever under the trees and I could hardly see.

The wings must have been torn off when the plane struck the trees and there was nothing left of the cockpit but a heap of sodden ash and some twisted metal. I cracked my right shin on something solid that didn't move and swore silently. The engine block. I stepped sideways to avoid it and bumped into something else.

I had heard about people's hearts coming into their mouths and dismissed it as absurd, a hack writer's cliché. That moment shattered my disbelief. I stood there too shocked to move while every instinct urged me to run.

For what I had backed into was soft and gave slightly under the impact.

A body.

I waited for the inevitable challenge. Maybe a blow. All I heard was a startled gasp. A woman's.

For several seconds neither of us moved. The silence, almost tangible now, was somehow menacing. Then she said in a low whisper, "Who are you?"

It was too quiet for me to recognise the voice and I didn't answer. If this was Stephanie Bridgeman I didn't want her knowing who it was snooping round her father's wood.

Then a lot of things started happening almost simultaneously. She switched on a torch and shone it on me. After the darkness the light was like a physical blow and I shielded my eyes.

"Mr. Fordham!"

Apart from that anguished cry I had never heard Stephanie Bridgeman speak but I knew this voice. It was Rekha Graham's.

At that moment a shotgun blasted the silence.

FIVE

The explosion shattered the quiet night. Beside me Mrs. Graham gasped. But she had the presence of mind to switch off her torch.

Almost without thinking I threw myself on her, pushing her away from the plane and back into the shelter of the trees. She stumbled and nearly fell but I grabbed her in time.

"What are you doing?" she demanded in a fierce undertone.

"Getting out of here," I told her. Whoever had fired that shot wasn't far away and I didn't intend being around if he fired again.

I found her arm and dragged her farther into the wood. Though she muttered in protest she didn't resist. She couldn't have fancied being shot at either. The trees were mostly beeches and there wasn't much undergrowth, so we could move fairly easily even in the darkness but I was uneasily aware of the lack of much real cover. If the man with a gun had a torch it wouldn't take him long to find us.

Who was he? Bridgeman? Foskett?

"Where's your car?" I whispered.

"In a lay-by."

I knew where she must mean. There was only one lay-by along the lane between the main road and the village. It was halfway down the first hill, about three hundred yards to our left, the last two hundred of them across open ground.

I could hear footsteps behind us now, a man's heavy tread on the hard turf. They were too close for comfort.

"Come on," I whispered urgently.

If the wood had been thicker we could have headed for the lane, keeping in the trees for longer. As it was there was nothing for it but to make for the far side as fast as we could. The sound of footsteps had given way to the rustle of leaves. Twigs snapped. Our pursuer, whoever he was, had reached the wood. Already we were almost at the other side and beyond it there was nothing but the bare slope down to the hedge.

We plunged on, the thick carpet of leaves dragging at our feet. My hand still grasped Mrs. Graham's arm and my heart was pounding. I glanced back over my shoulder and saw a torch shining on the trees but it was too far away for the light to reach us. Twice we blundered into trees and stopped, shaken, before we charged on again.

Then suddenly the darkness lightened a little and we emerged onto the grassy slope.

"Make for your car," I whispered. "I'll try to draw him off."

I daresay it sounded like false heroics but it made sense. Whoever was behind couldn't follow both of us and if he heard me go straight on, the odds were he would stick to me. I could run faster alone while, by keeping to the edge of the wood, Mrs. Graham would have a good chance of reaching her car without being spotted.

Unless there were two of them.

She didn't wait to argue. The clouds were more broken now and after the darkness under the trees it seemed appallingly light. I ran on, wondering how long a start I had.

Two or three times I stumbled and nearly fell. I was reasonably fit but even so I was soon gasping for breath. At first I made straight for the hedge, intent on putting as much distance between myself and the man with the gun as I could before he emerged from the wood. I couldn't hear him now, the only sounds were the soft pounding of my plimsolls on the turf and the beating of my heart. But maybe I only felt that.

I had covered a hundred yards or so before I realised he might assume I had come from the road and go that way. I was fairly confident I could outpace Bridgeman or Foskett but I doubted if Mrs. Graham could. What would they do if they caught her? Trespassing in itself wasn't a crime but I couldn't forget that shot.

Breathlessly I shouted, "This way," hoping whoever it was would assume we were still together. Perhaps he didn't know there were two of us.

"Stop! You there, stop!" Foskett's voice.

I charged on, swerving to the left, then to the right, zigzagging down the hill. Once I looked back and saw a pinpoint of light in the darkness.

Then Foskett fired again. He couldn't have seen more than a moving shadow, if that, and he was probably a good hundred yards behind me, but shot spreads and I didn't fancy being peppered with it.

By now I could make out the dark line of the hedge. There was a stunted tree twenty yards or so to the left of the thinner patch and I ran straight towards it.

This time I hardly noticed the stinging twigs. I pushed through and started running to the left, round the edge of the field. When I had gone thirty yards or so I flung myself down into the wheat, burrowing into it, hoping the corn would close over me. I lay there panting and praying that now I was off Bridgeman's land Foskett would give up the chase.

Somewhere away to the left a car started. I looked up through the wheat and saw headlights coming down the lane. Rekha Graham had made it. But if she came to the farm Foskett would know who it was that had been poking round the wreckage of her husband's plane. He wouldn't have got home yet.

Hardly breathing, I watched the lights sweep up the second rise. They passed the end of the track and I drew a sigh of relief. Yet perversely I was disappointed. I had wanted to find out why she had been in the wood; now I might never know.

I waited a few minutes longer, then decided to chance it. Getting to my feet, I walked back to the edge of the field. All was quiet.

I took my time climbing the slope and crossing the meadow. My legs felt weak. I told myself it was the exertion, I wasn't used to so much running, but I knew that was only part of the truth; I had been scared.

A shadow moved in the yard and I stopped, nerves on edge.

"You've been a long time," Rekha Graham said.

I relaxed again. It was absurd to be so pleased she was here. "I didn't fancy being shot at again," I retorted. "It might have been third time lucky."

"I was afraid something had happened to you."

So she had been concerned. We went into the house and I switched on the light. Brandy ambled over and she stooped to pat him. She was wearing a thin sweater and jeans; it was the first time I had seen her in Western dress.

"I thought you'd gone home," I told her. "I saw the lights go past."

"I turned round in the village and came back without them in case somebody was still watching."

An intelligent young woman, Rekha Graham, I thought. And cool.

Her hair was coming loose and she put up a hand to straighten it. There was blood on her arm.

"You've scratched yourself," I said.

"The first shot hit me. It isn't much."

I was startled. Then I remembered how she had gasped. I took her arm and rolled up her sleeve. There was a tiny wound just above her elbow.

"You'd better get that seen to," I told her. "Does it hurt?"

"Not much. There are some more in my leg. You aren't proposing to look at those too, are you?" She sounded amused.

I remembered that I had half dragged, half pushed her through the wood and she hadn't complained. "I'll get you a drink, then we'll go to the hospital," I told her.

I expected her to protest but suddenly she looked exhausted. She let me take her through to the living-room and sit her down in one of the easy chairs while I poured her a large whisky. Neat. She drank it, grimacing.

"Who was it?" she asked. "Do you know?"

"Foskett. He's Bridgeman's manager."

"I heard you shout. He fired again just as I got to the hedge and I was afraid he had hit you."

Suddenly she shivered uncontrollably.

"I'm going to take you to hospital," I said.

"There's no need." A little of her former spirit had returned. "I'm quite capable of driving myself."

"Perhaps you are," I agreed. "But you don't know where it is and you'd probably pass out before you found it. There won't be many people to ask at this time of night."

She stood up as if to prove she could manage. For a second she swayed, then she pulled herself together.

"Thank you for the drink, Mr. Fordham. And for helping me."

"Don't be silly," I told her. "I'm going to drive you."

She regarded me steadily, an expression I couldn't fathom in her eyes. "Thank you then," she agreed. "Perhaps it would be more sensible."

For her that was quite an admission.

We went in her Jaguar because it was parked by the house and my car was locked in the barn. I had never driven a car like that before and at first I went carefully. But by the time we reached the main road I had got the feel of it and was beginning to enjoy myself. Only the necessity of getting her to hospital as quickly as possible marred my pleasure.

The casualty officer was an Indian. She said something to him in a language that might have been Chinese for all I understood and he nodded, grinning. Then they took her off to one of the cubicles. Apparently there weren't any other casualties just then.

"What will you do?" she asked, turning to look at me before the swing doors closed behind them.

"Wait," I said.

"There's no need. Take my car—I can get a taxi home."

If they let her out tonight, I thought. How badly was her leg hurt? Moreover I had an idea that hospitals were obliged to report all firearms injuries and that would mean questions. Probably the police. Added to all of which there was only one taxi firm in Stallford. They didn't operate a twenty-four-hour service and I doubted if they would be very keen on turning out to drive her to Hampstead in the wee small hours.

Of course the hospital might send her in an ambulance.

"I'll wait," I said.

She shrugged as if she thought I was stupid and followed the doctor and nurse. Maybe she was woman enough to like having a man hang around her. Even me. Mousy-haired, with glasses and few of the social graces, I didn't flatter myself that I was any woman's dream of masculine perfection.

They kept her a long time. I had read all the magazines in the waiting area, even the women's, before she came back with the doctor. She looked more tired than ever but she said, "That's done," briskly enough.

I looked at the doctor. "You're not going to keep her in?"

He smiled faintly. I guessed there had been an argument about it and she, inevitably, had won. The nurse looked disapproving.

We went out to the car. This time she didn't suggest that she drive and I noticed she got in rather awkwardly, but I knew better by now than to say anything. I drove out into the street past the rows of silent houses. We were nearly halfway back to the farm before either of us spoke, then I asked, "What did you tell them?"

"That I was cleaning a gun and it went off."

I was flabbergasted. "At this time of night? And they believed you?"

"I couldn't think of anything else. I think they suspected you fired it."

We were rounding a bend and I couldn't look at her face but I had an idea she was smiling. Like Queen Victoria, I wasn't amused. Perhaps I was just too tired.

"I'm hardly surprised," I told her, fighting back my annoyance. After all, I lived in the district.

"You needn't worry. I told them you weren't there: I was staying at your house but you weren't in the room when it happened."

I still felt stunned. "If they report it to the police they'll come round asking questions."

"Would that matter?"

"It's a serious matter to lie to the police."

"People do it every day. They must get used to it." She

sounded amused. After a moment she added more seriously, "I could hardly tell them we were snooping in
Bridgeman's wood."

If you were cleaning a gun and it went off, you were likely
to get a good deal more than a single pellet in an arm and a
few in a leg. She hadn't thought of that. I wondered if the
doctor had.

"They would have thought we were snogging," she said.

Coming from her, the expression was startling. And this
time there was no mistaking her amusement. I laughed, I
couldn't help it. Maybe it was relief, the reaction after all
that had happened. I felt relaxed and realised how tense I
had been before.

We turned off the main road. Was Bridgeman asleep over
there in his big house? And Foskett? He lived in a cottage
on the farm with his wife, a sour-looking woman, and a boy
of about six. Perhaps he was still prowling about in case the
snoopers returned. I wondered what he had been so afraid
we would find.

Fifty years of traffic had worn the track to my house fairly
smooth, but still the big car pitched and rolled a little. I
heard Mrs. Graham catch her breath quickly and guessed
the jolting wasn't doing her leg much good.

"Sorry," I said.

I stopped in front of the house. I wasn't sure how to tell
her. She wouldn't like it, she might even take it the wrong
way, but I couldn't help that.

She beat me to it. "Thank you, Mr. Fordham." Her tone
was very matter-of-fact. She might have been thanking me
for handing her a drink. "It was very kind of you to take me
to the hospital and to wait for me but now I must go home."
Unnecessarily she added, "It's very late."

"You can't drive home like that," I told her.

"Then what do you propose I do? I can hardly go to a hotel."

"You're going to stay here."

I saw her turn her head but her face was in shadow.

"Thank you, but that's out of the question."

"If you think I'm going to let you drive to London with that leg—" I began.

"I'll manage perfectly well. It's not very far."

"Thirty miles. Last night you said it was a long way."

"To ask me a lot of questions, yes. Will you get out, please?"

"No," I said. I didn't care if she suspected my motives. After all, she couldn't know I didn't like her very much.

Suddenly, surprisingly, she laughed. "What would people say?"

"They won't know."

It was probably untrue but I doubted if people's knowing would worry her very much. Anyway, she didn't live here.

We sat there, neither of us speaking. I was determined and she couldn't very well push me out if I wouldn't go; I'm six feet and weigh thirteen stone.

"I suppose I have no choice," she said at last.

"No."

"Very well then." No thanks.

She opened the door and started to get out. This time she couldn't stifle a quick little gasp of pain. I went round to her side and helped her.

Brandy didn't get up when I switched on the light. Perhaps he was resigned to strange comings and goings tonight. I saw Mrs. Graham was sitting fairly comfortably and went upstairs to the spare room. Luckily the bed was always made up. It wasn't unknown for one of my friends to drop in for the evening and decide it was better to spend the night there than in a police cell with the prospect of losing his licence. I fetched a towel from the airing cupboard, put it on the rail in the bathroom and went back downstairs.

Her eyes were closed. Off guard her face looked drawn and I guessed the shot had hurt a good deal. Probably removing it too. She heard me and opened her eyes.

"I hope there's everything you need," I told her. "I'm afraid I don't keep a stock of nightdresses."

She smiled. "I could wear a pair of your pyjamas."

Perhaps she wasn't serious. After all, she was only about five feet four and slender. I guessed she would look very appealing in them with her hair loose. The trouble was, I wouldn't see her.

"I'll get some," I said.

"I don't like sleeping in jeans."

When I came back with the pyjamas she held them against herself and laughed. The bottoms of the legs hung several inches on the floor.

"Will anyone be worried if you don't go home?" I asked. Then I could have kicked myself. What business was it of mine? If she had wanted to phone she could have done so from the hospital or asked.

Her eyes were blank. "No." The slightest of pauses before she added, "I live alone."

"I'm sorry, I didn't mean—" I began.

"It doesn't matter."

She refused coffee and we went upstairs. I showed her the spare bedroom and the bathroom.

"Thank you," she said.

"Good night then." Why did I feel awkward? I was thirty, had been married, it wasn't as if I had never had much to do with women.

"Good night, Mr. Fordham." Her tone was cool, almost remote.

Hell! I thought. If she regarded me as a clumsy oaf it was

my own fault. And I had seen her in a new light tonight. She had courage. And a sense of humour. That was something I hadn't suspected.

I went back downstairs and made myself some coffee, giving her time to finish in the bathroom. When I went to bed a quarter of an hour later her light was out.

SIX

I was awakened by sunlight streaming in at the window. Normally I was up by six-thirty; this morning when I looked at the clock it was eight-forty-five. I jumped out of bed, remembered Rekha Graham just in time, and pulled on a pair of trousers before I went along to the bathroom. Just as well—she emerged from it at the same moment. She was wearing my pyjamas. The bottoms of the trousers were rolled up several inches but still they nearly swamped her. Without any makeup and with her hair down she looked about fourteen.

"Good morning, Mr. Fordham." Her eyes were mischievous. "Do you think they suit me?"

"Very well," I said, fighting an insane desire to put my arms round her. "Did you sleep all right?"

"Yes, thank you."

"How's your leg this morning?"

"A bit sore, that's all."

I guessed she was making light of it. It probably hurt like hell.

"When I've shaved I'll get some breakfast," I said.

"Could I just have some fruit juice?"

"Yes of course, if you're sure."

"It's all I ever have in the morning."

"Right then," I agreed.

When I went downstairs a quarter of an hour later she was already there, hair done and face made up, making a fuss of Brandy. He was lapping it up disgracefully. I decided it wouldn't do me any harm to skip the bacon and eggs for once, poured two glasses of orange juice and took them through to the living room. There was a tablecloth in one of the sideboard drawers and I spread it over the table. Mrs. Graham watched me in silence.

"We'd better have a talk," I told her.

"Oh?"

Clearly she had no intention of making it easy for me.

"What were you doing in the wood last night?"

Our eyes met. Hers were challenging. But I was determined not to give way.

"What were you?" she asked evenly.

"I couldn't sleep. I thought it would be a good idea to have a look before they carted the wreckage away."

"Just that?"

"More or less."

"So did I."

"Thirty miles is a long way to come in the middle of the night just to look round," I said. It seemed a good point.

There was quite a pause before she remarked, "You made me curious."

"I'm curious too. About a lot of things. Bridgeman is supposed to have some sort of business in London, I'd like to know what it is."

"It's a small art gallery. Just off Bond Street."

My surprise must have shown. "You said you didn't know him," I reminded her.

"I don't. I'd never met him until the other day. But I know the gallery."

"Is it crooked?"

She smiled faintly. "Ask some artists and they'll tell you all galleries are crooked. I've never heard anything against it. You still think Derek was going to see him, don't you?"

"Yes."

"And that they were both involved in something crooked."

"I think it's possible." I sipped my orange juice. It had a clean, sharp tang. "If there was something on the plane Bridgeman didn't want found, that would explain why he took so long to call the fire service. He made sure it was going to be completely destroyed first."

"What could there have been?"

"I don't know," I admitted. "That's why I went to have a look last night, I thought there was just a chance I might find something."

"I found this."

She reached in the pocket of her jeans and brought out a small piece of cloth about three inches by two. I took it. The fabric looked like canvas. The edges were charred but although it had been soaked in water it was still fairly stiff. I thought I could see traces of colour on one side but they were too faint to be sure.

"It looks as if it came from the plane," I commented.

"Yes, I suppose so."

She put it back in her pocket. I didn't like the careful way she handled it. What sort of woman could treasure a souvenir from the plane in which her husband had died, even if she had disliked him? Yet she hadn't seemed hard last night.

"Do you think that man Foskett was trying to kill us?" she asked.

I shook my head. "I shouldn't think so. He was probably just trying to scare us off. He couldn't have counted on hitting us in the dark and at that range."

"So it was just luck."

"Bad luck," I agreed.

"I suppose that's something we should be thankful for."

But Foskett would have told Bridgeman by now and they would have a pretty good idea who had been in the wood. Knowing that didn't make me feel any better.

Mrs. Graham finished her orange juice and stood up. Awkwardly. No doubt her leg was heavily bandaged.

"Thank you for all you did last night," she said. "And for making me stay. I'm sorry to have been so much trouble."

Her tone was coolly formal and I felt clumsy again.

"You couldn't have driven home," I told her.

"No."

She picked up her handbag and we went out to her car. I noticed her grimace as she tucked her left leg in.

"Are you sure you're fit to drive now?" I asked.

"Are you offering to chauffeur me again?" She smiled with a hint of the mischief I had seen before. Then she opened her handbag and took out a card. "If you should ever want to get in touch with me during the day you can get me here."

I took the card and glanced at it. It bore the name of one of the most famous auction houses in London. In the world. Underneath were the words *"Mrs. Rekha Graham, Director."* I stared at it stupidly.

By the time I looked up again she had started the engine and the car was moving away along the track. I stuffed the card in my pocket and walked back into the house.

She could have told me her number while we were indoors where I could write it down. Instead she had chosen this way. To put me in my place. It was a deliberate brush-off—and not very subtle at that. What right had she to suppose I would want to get in touch with her? As far as I was concerned the business was over. I didn't care for running in the dark with somebody taking pot shots at me. Or lying on my belly in cornfields. I wasn't sure I cared much for Rekha Graham either.

So why did I keep remembering her leaning on me with my arm round her last night? And the sight of her in my pyjamas looking so ridiculously young and defenceless?

The trouble was, I thought, I was starved of feminine company and she was too bloody attractive. She knew it, too. I couldn't blame her for that, but if she thought I wouldn't be able to resist calling her she was mistaken. I had no intention of seeing her again. Especially now. The sooner my life returned to normal the better.

I did some tidying up, washed yesterday's dirty crockery and went out to the barn. But I couldn't settle to anything for long and knowing why didn't help. In the end I called Brandy and went for a walk.

When I got back I found my sister-in-law's car parked in front of the house. Sighing, I went indoors.

Elizabeth was looking out of the living-room window. She was a well-built woman and if it hadn't been for her permanently embittered expression she would have been quite attractive. As it was, most of the time she was being either condescending or complaining. Sometimes both at once.

Her father had been a prominent man in the district, chairman of the council and the local N.F.U., and Elizabeth's mother had made the most of her role in local society. Old Mannion wasn't a bad sort but he was inclined to be pompous and I daresay he enjoyed it too. They must have regarded Peter as the ideal son-in-law. The elder son of one of the most prosperous farmers in the area, moderately good-looking, well-mannered, popular with almost everybody. It must have been a terrible shock when he decided his inclinations lay in a different direction and his only ambition was to see how quickly he could empty a bottle of scotch. To do her justice, I don't think that had anything to do with Elizabeth. Strangely, she seemed to believe that in some way it was my fault. I suppose she had to blame somebody.

"Do you know where Peter is?" she demanded when I walked in.

"I've no idea," I answered. I was accustomed to her implying I kept him hidden from her. I would have done if he had asked me, but he never did.

"I thought he might be with you," she said accusingly.

"I haven't seen him for days," I assured her. "How long has he been gone?"

"Since just after ten."

"Damn it," I protested. "That isn't long." But I knew we were both thinking the same thing: he had been in time for the pubs to open. The odds were he was on another bender. Weekends were always the worst; the rest of the week he at least made a pretence of working on the farm our father had left him. Luckily he had a good foreman. Even so, the place was going downhill pretty fast.

I glanced at my watch. It was just after one-thirty. Time for him to be so drunk he was incapable. The bloody fool. But he was forty-four; if he wanted to drink himself stupid there wasn't much I could do about it.

I realised I was hungry. I hadn't had anything since last night except a glass of orange juice.

"He'll be home soon," I said encouragingly.

When the Cross Keys closed. Unless he had gone to the Feathers. They were his usual haunts. It was one reason why I used the Red Lion. And old Mathers at the Feathers would go on serving him as long as he paid. One of these days he would get run in, driving home in that state. I only hoped he wouldn't kill somebody first.

"We're supposed to be going to the Bridgemans' this evening," Elizabeth said resentfully. "Eunice is having a few friends in for a party. He knows I want to go; I promised her we would."

"Hard luck," I sympathised. It was news to me they knew the Bridgemans.

My sister-in-law eyed me thoughtfully. Then, a pleading note in her voice I had hardly ever heard before, she asked, "Would you come with me, Clive? If Peter can't?"

"Me?" I could hardly believe I had heard her right. She knew only too well that I hated cocktail parties. When Pat and I were first married she had done her best to involve us in her social life and I suspected she had never forgiven us for our lack of interest. Nevertheless she had been kind to Pat and they had got on surprisingly well. Kind to me too after Pat died.

"Yes," she said.

"You must be joking."

She looked offended. "That's not very polite."

"I'm sorry, Elizabeth, I didn't mean it like that. But you know how I feel about cocktail parties. Why don't you go alone?"

"No thank you."

I grinned. In her eyes going without her husband wouldn't matter but going without a man would be tantamount to an admission of failure. Almost a social gaffe.

Perhaps after all it might not be such a bad idea for me to take her. I was bound to see a lot of people I knew. Not close friends, but the Bridgemans would see I mixed with those they probably considered the right people. I had friends here; they were the ones who were alone. And I might have an opportunity to hint to Bridgeman that I hadn't been the trespasser in his wood last night. At least I would be able to watch him at close quarters.

I had forgotten my resolve that for me the whole business was over and done with.

"All right," I agreed. "If Peter can't go, give me a ring and I'll take you."

It can't have sounded exactly gracious, put like that, but Elizabeth was too relieved to care.

"Bless you, Clive," she said. "We're supposed to be there some time after six-thirty; I'll give you a ring about four."

To my astonishment she kissed me and walked to the door.

"You'll like the Bridgemans," she said. "I've only met him once but Peter says he's all right. And Eunice is sweet."

"What about Stephanie?" I asked, grinning.

"Oh well. But she's hardly ever there. It's time you got to know Harry and Eunice—they are your nearest neighbours."

"Yes," I agreed.

After Elizabeth had gone I got myself some lunch. As usual when I was alone, I ate it in the kitchen with the morning paper propped up in front of me.

I spent the afternoon catching up on some paperwork and half hoping she would ring to say thank you very much but Peter had come home surprisingly sober and was going to take her. My going in his place didn't seem such a good idea now. The farther I kept from the Bridgemans for the time being the better.

But when the phone rang just after four she said Peter wasn't feeling very well and could I call for her about six-thirty? I cursed my brother silently and promised I would.

SEVEN

The Bridgemans' house had been built in the seventeenth century of that lovely mellow red brick that builders used then. A small manor house at the time, it was large by modern standards. Before Bridgeman bought Langley Farm it had belonged to a man named Ellis who was the chairman of a big engineering company. He had acquired it in the fifties when a lot of wealthy businessmen were buying farms and deliberately running them at a loss for tax reasons. He was a likeable man and the local people regarded him with a mixture of tolerance and irritation. They didn't much care for that sort of farming.

The house was screened on both sides by trees, fine old oaks and elms that towered over it, and I wondered if they were what had attracted Bridgeman to it. Then I saw something else and knew they weren't. Or only as a secondary advantage.

Ellis had tarmacked the long drive from the main road. At first it climbed gradually but for the last three or four hundred yards it ran along a sort of ledge just below the crest of the rise. Driving along it with Elizabeth I suddenly saw what had puzzled me before; the drive was a ready-made runway. That was what Bridgeman had liked about the place. Graham had been trying to land there, not on the meadow beside it, but in the fading light he had miscalculated, overshot it and crashed into the wood just beyond.

"You're very silent," my sister-in-law remarked reprovingly. "You will try to be sociable when we get there, won't you, Clive?"

"I'll be at my most charming," I promised. Elizabeth would be surprised.

She gave me a suspicious look but evidently decided it would be wiser not to say anything more. She was probably still wondering why I had agreed to bring her.

I tagged the Ford onto the end of a line of cars that seemed to comprise Rolls and Jaguars with the odd Rover and BMW. They made me feel like a poor relation and I suspected Elizabeth was wishing she had suggested we come in Peter's Rover. If I had thought about it I might have given the Cortina a wash down that afternoon, if only for her sake; it was filthy.

The heavy oak front door was open and a middle-aged woman in a green dress and an apron told us everybody was on the terrace. We crossed the hall to a big drawing-room with french windows, its walls hung with several paintings. They were mostly landscapes and I walked across to study one more closely. It was a river scene, the stream bounded by wide, flat meadows under a threatening sky done in the style of the Impressionists. Then I saw the signature "E. Bridgeman" in the bottom left-hand corner. I couldn't have explained why I was surprised.

There must have been at least fifty people on the terrace, and as many more talking on the lawn. They were a mixed crowd—obvious businessmen and their wives, local people and a sprinkling of the determinedly artistic. I saw several familiar faces but nobody I particularly wanted to talk to and, in any case, they were busy talking to other people already. Another waitress dressed identically to the one who had greeted us in the hall came up carrying a tray and we helped ourselves to drinks. I settled for white wine on the grounds that it was cooler and more refreshing; Elizabeth took a sherry.

"There are the Hoopers," she remarked suddenly. "I must speak to Shirley. I'll see you later, Clive. And do talk to people."

I knew the Hoopers slightly—he was an estate agent in Stallford—but I felt no inclination to join them. I was looking for Bridgeman.

He was on the lawn talking to a stocky, middle-aged man in a suit that was too bright for the occasion. He looked out of place there. One of Bridgeman's business friends from London dressed for the country, I supposed.

I turned away and saw Mrs. Bridgeman. I knew her by sight although we had never spoken to each other. She noticed me at the same moment, murmured something to her companions and walked over. Eunice Bridgeman was still an attractive woman and it was easy to see where Stephanie got her looks. They had the same blond colouring and build, though her mother's figure was a little thicker now and her hair was probably tinted. There was a calmness about her it was hard to imagine Stephanie ever possessing if what I had heard was true. Very likely it wasn't. A hint of strength too.

"You're Clive Fordham, aren't you?" she said.

This native, at least, sounded friendly. I explained Peter wasn't very well so I had come with Elizabeth and I hoped it was all right.

"Of course it is; I'm very glad you did. I hope it's nothing serious?"

"No, he's just taken something that hasn't agreed with him." Strictly the truth, I told myself, however she interpreted it. "I expect he'll be all right tomorrow."

"There's so much of that sort of thing going round just

now," she agreed sympathetically. If she knew about Peter she concealed it well.

Another waitress brought us a tray loaded with canapés and tiny sausage rolls. I took a sausage roll. It was good. "You must come and meet Harry," my hostess told me. She hadn't taken anything; maybe she was dieting. "You don't know each other, do you? He's hardly ever here; he gets home from town late and then he has to go away on business a lot."

"We've met, that's about all," I said. Apparently Bridgeman hadn't told her about the other night.

He was still talking to the man in the loud suit, a little apart from the rest of the party. His wife led me over to them, exchanging polite nothings with other guests as we passed. I caught Elizabeth's eye and saw her give me a little nod of approval. She didn't know half of it, I thought.

"Harry," Eunice said gaily, "you don't know Clive Fordham properly, do you?"

His cold little eyes stared at me. No friendliness there.

"We met the other night," he replied.

"When that plane crashed," I explained. "I heard it and came over to see if there was anything I could do."

"Wasn't it terrible?" Eunice's face clouded. "That poor man."

Her husband ignored her and turned to his companion. "This is Lew Fucillo." We shook hands. "Fordham has the next farm. Over there." He jerked his head in the direction of the wood.

"Is that so?" Fucillo looked interested. He had a strong American accent. New York, I guessed; certainly not the South. He was at least a stone and a half overweight but there was nothing soft about him—a pretty tough business-man, I decided. But his manner was pleasant enough now. Maybe I had misjudged him.

"Lew's a picture dealer in New York," Bridgeman explained. "He's over here on business."

"That's right. Just for a few days. Do you know anything about pictures, Mr. Fordham?"

"Very little," I admitted.

"It's a fascinating business."

"Big business too, isn't it?" I suggested.

He grinned complacently. "Sure. But I'm a businessman, I enjoy it."

I wondered which had priority, art or business, and thought I knew the answer.

Eunice Bridgeman laughed. Then she excused herself to talk to some of her other guests. I told myself I should be trying to find out more about her husband and his gallery but if I asked too many questions I would arouse his suspicions and, anyway, it was difficult with the American there.

"You have a gallery in London, I believe?" I remarked innocently.

"Yes." Bridgeman nodded curtly.

"A very fine one," Fucillo said. "Very fine indeed. We do a lot of business together."

"It has a good reputation," Bridgeman agreed.

He had spoken pompously and for the first time it occurred to me that he was vain. Perhaps that explained a good deal; some people claimed crime was a form of vanity. And his vanity was of that sort—not the weak, laughable self-regard of ordinary conceit but hard and dangerous. It made me feel uneasy.

"Do you have any trouble with poachers?" he demanded suddenly.

I was startled. "No," I answered. "Why?"

"Foskett found a couple up by the wood there last night."

He was watching me too closely for comfort and I hoped

my expression hadn't given anything away. The sudden challenge had almost caught me off guard.

"What were they after?" I enquired.

"Christ knows. Foskett put the fear of God in them; I shouldn't think they'll come back. If anybody thinks he can come messing about on my land as if it was his own he'll soon find how wrong he is."

"Foskett caught them then?"

"No."

Was he warning me off? It was hard to tell. But I was pretty sure he suspected I had been one of the "poachers."

"There's nothing much for them on my land," I remarked lightly.

"Foskett said they made off your way."

"I didn't hear anything. What time was it?"

"About one."

I forced a grin. Hoped it looked more natural than it felt. "I was asleep long before then."

"The best place to be," Fucillo agreed, smiling. I wondered what he thought of his host's attitude.

We chatted for a few more minutes, then I decided I wasn't going to learn any more and muttered something about wondering if I could get myself another drink. Bridgeman told me I'd find one on the terrace but made no move to get it for me. I wandered off. He seemed hardly to notice my going.

I found one of the waitresses and helped myself to another glass of wine. It was nearly lukewarm. When I looked round again the American had gone and Bridgeman was talking to Stephanie. She was wearing a yellow dress that made the most of her figure and revealed a good deal of it. I saw her nod once or twice as if she was being given instructions and look in my direction. I told myself I was letting my imagination run away with me; probably it was nothing more sinister than what to do when the guests had gone. Some people I knew came along and we talked. When they drifted away I sipped my wine and wondered how much longer Elizabeth would expect to stay. She was in a group farther along the terrace, standing next to Lady Denson, the lord lieutenant's wife.

"Hallo there," a voice said behind me in a bright drawl. It was Stephanie. At close range the effect of the yellow dress was more striking than ever.

"Hallo," I said.

"I've been hoping I could talk to you. We've never met properly." Her voice was light, slightly affected, modulated in the way her drama school had taught her.

"You were upset the last time," I said.

"Yes." Her lovely face clouded as her mother's had done. "I thought for one awful moment that poor man in the plane was somebody I knew."

"What made you think that?" I asked.

Her eyes, wide, regarded me steadily. They were an unusually deep blue, shaded by feathery false lashes. "I don't know. Shock, I suppose. I didn't think straight."

"But it wasn't?"

"No, thank God. That sounds dreadfully heartless, doesn't it?"

"Not really."

She smiled brilliantly. For no reason at all I thought of Rekha Graham's smile, the spark of mischief in her eyes, and wished I hadn't.

"It must be nice having friends who drop in by plane," I suggested.

"Oh, they don't." She said it a shade too quickly. "I just thought he might. He has his own plane."

"What's his name?" I asked, as casually as I could.

"Ritchie Broome. He lives in London." She paused. "Daddy was terribly upset there was nothing he could do."

"I'm sure he was," I agreed.

"He had the men search the next day. In case there was anything he could hand over to that poor woman."

"I shouldn't think there was much left after the fire," I commented, amused by her description of Rekha Graham.

"No, there wasn't. You didn't find anything, did you?"

So that was what her father had been telling her, to find out if I had picked up anything that night. He must have reckoned I was more likely to tell her than him if I had. But she hadn't been exactly subtle about it.

"No, nothing," I answered. The lie didn't trouble my conscience. "It was too dark to see much and I wasn't looking."

"No."

Was it my imagination or did she sound relieved?

"It was just one of those things that happen," I told her. "An accident. It was terrible but there's nothing anybody can do about it now."

"One has to look at it like that, I know," she agreed.

I hoped she would report what I had said to her father. With luck he might even believe it.

"You're an actress, aren't you?" I asked her, changing the subject. "Are you in anything just now?"

"We start rehearsals for a new play at Watford next week." She proceeded to tell me all about the play, then about people with whom she had acted, dropping well-known names with a casualness that wouldn't have deceived a child. I wondered if she was just being her age or if her father had told her to keep me talking. I didn't much care, it passed the time and at least she was good to look at.

Twice I noticed her glance at her watch. Eventually she said, "It's been super meeting you, Clive. I'd love to stay but if I don't go and talk to some of the other people the parents will start getting uptight."

She flashed me another brilliant smile and I watched her thread her way between the chattering groups and disappear into the house. Who did she expect to find in there?

One of the waitresses returned and I helped myself to another sausage roll and a chicken *vol-au-vent*. The heat and the wine were making me thirsty and I could have done with a long, cool pint of beer. But Elizabeth was still in the little group clustered round Lady Denson and I knew she wouldn't be pleased if I said I wanted to leave.

I looked across the lawn. Bridgeman was talking to an elegant dark girl in a cream dress. One of his London friends, I guessed; I was pretty sure she wasn't local. His wife was farther along the terrace, listening patiently to a small, elderly woman with a peculiarly penetrating voice. Nobody was taking any notice of me. I put my empty glass down on one of the tables and slipped through the french windows.

After the heat on the terrace the drawing-room was pleasantly cool. Also, it was deserted. I walked across to the hall door. The waitress who had greeted us when we arrived had gone but the front door was still open, presumably for the benefit of any guests who might still come.

A man was going up the stairs. There was something surreptitious about him and with a little shock of surprise I recognised Foskett. Then a girl's voice somewhere on the landing above my head whispered urgently, "Come on, we haven't long." Stephanie. I waited until I heard a bedroom door close quietly behind them, then I crossed the hall and went out by the front door. It looked as if what they said in the village was true.

There was a hum of conversation from the terrace and I turned left away from it. On this side were the old stables, a two-storied building Ellis had converted into a garage. The old doors had been taken out and replaced with a wide up-and-over contraption. I was prepared to bet it was fitted with one of those remote control devices which enable you to open the door without getting out of your car.

I turned left again. Behind the garage there were two smaller buildings. The first one looked like a toolshed; there were some loose slates on the roof and the brickwork badly needed repointing. Nobody had followed me, so I walked up to the window and looked in. Gardening tools were hanging from brackets and propped against the walls.

The second outbuilding had been restored. Patches of new bricks showed raw in the old walls, the roof had been reslated and the door was new. It looked surprisingly solid for a workshed and there was a Yale lock. But the work must have been done several weeks ago at least; the roof was liberally daubed with bird droppings. I wondered why Bridgeman had had this shed repaired and left the other.

Then I realised there was another difference between them; this one had no window. A square of new bricks marked where it had been. Perhaps Bridgeman was an en-thusiastic amateur photographer and this was his dark-room. Perhaps, but it seemed unlikely. I couldn't imagine him or his family taking an interest in photography.

I turned. Somebody was standing by the side of the ga-rage watching me. The dark girl who had been talking to Bridgeman when I left the terrace. She didn't move, just stood there watching me. There was something almost menacing about her stillness and the way she stared at me. Had Bridgeman sent her to see where I went? The vague uneasiness I had felt earlier returned.

"Why, Clive!"

Startled by the voice behind me, I turned. Eunice was standing a few yards away. She must have come round the corner of the house while I was looking at the girl. Now she came towards me, smiling.

"I'm sorry, I'm afraid I was looking round your garden," I told her. "Elizabeth's talking to some of her friends."

"Oh dear!" Eunice laughed. "It is rather nice, isn't it? Bob Slater does most of it and he's wonderful but I enjoy pottering about."

To my surprise she tucked her arm in mine and led me towards a corner some distance from the house where the formal beds gave way to massed flowers with clumps of rhododendrons behind them.

"This is my favourite spot."

"It's lovely," I said truthfully.

"I'm glad you think so too. Harry and Stephanie are bored stiff with gardens but I love them."

She smiled, a private, rather secretive smile. I found myself liking her and wondering how she had come to marry a man like her husband. Yet she seemed happy.

I glanced back. The dark girl had gone.

"Have you a dog?" I asked.

"No. Why?"

"It just seems the sort of house where you almost expect to find dogs," I explained.

"Harry doesn't like them. Steph wanted one when we came here but he said no. I think it's rather a pity."

We strolled on towards the terrace. Just before we reached it she excused herself to speak to a couple who were looking for her. I helped myself to another glass of wine and watched the crowd on the terrace. It was beginning to thin as people drifted away. I decided I had done my duty and now it was time for Elizabeth to reciprocate. It took a pretty broad hint and I had to repeat it but in the end she came.

"I think we could have stayed a little longer," she complained as I backed the Cortina out of the line of cars. Already there were gaps. "There were several people I didn't have a chance to talk to."

It was on the tip of my tongue to point out that she would have had plenty of time if she hadn't spent so long hobnobbing with Lady Denson but my mother had taught me always to be polite to ladies so I let it pass.

"Don't you think I behaved well?" I asked cheerfully instead.

"At least you did talk to people some of the time," my sister-in-law conceded.

I grinned. I was thinking about the second of the two outbuildings. Would the dark girl tell Bridgeman she had found me looking at it?

EIGHT

Just before nine o'clock I strolled up to the village. Three cups of tea had failed to cure my thirst.

The Fox was a typical village pub. Not the sort you see on calendars but a plain whitewashed cottage with two rooms converted into bars and an extension built onto one side. Nearly all its customers were local people and I knew most of them. I stayed for an hour or so, talking and playing darts, then walked home. By ten-thirty I was in bed; I hadn't had much sleep the night before.

I slept soundly and woke about half-past seven. It was cloudy and a lot cooler with the threat of rain later. I dressed and went downstairs, pulling the paper out of the letter-box as I passed. Yesterday's breakfast had consisted of a glass of orange juice; today I was hungry.

I fried myself bacon, an egg, two sausages and a couple of tomatoes and grilled some toast, then ate it in the kitchen with the paper propped up against the marmalade jar. There wasn't much news—it was the silly season and the main stories wouldn't have made the front page on a good day. I took a mouthful of bacon and egg and turned over.

There was a report about corruption in a Midlands town and a scandal involving a female pop star all too obviously calculated to titillate readers. I wasn't titillated, just bored; perhaps there was something wrong with me. I turned another page.

A headline spread across several columns: "YARD SEEK

ART GANG." As there was nothing more interesting I read the story while I ate. It was a rehash of old reports—I had seen stories of thefts from big country houses as long as I could remember—but apparently this time it was different. The gang took only one or two pictures at a time and it looked as if they were directed by an expert; the paintings they stole weren't necessarily the ones which would have attracted an ordinary thief but they were always extremely valuable.

According to the paper, Scotland Yard believed the gang stole to order with a buyer for each picture before it was taken. Probably abroad. There were plenty of fanatical collectors ready to pay high prices for paintings they could never hang where they would be seen. It seemed strange to me they should be content to gloat over their treasures in secret, I had always thought half the pleasure in collecting was showing off one's possessions to other people. But presumably they had twisted minds.

One thing puzzling the police was how the paintings were smuggled out of the country. Several of them were large and they couldn't be folded. Nor could you tuck a picture five feet by four under your arm and carry it onto a plane. The most likely explanation was that they were sent out in cases containing perfectly legitimate goods.

I think it was the mention of planes that stirred my interest. You could take a pretty large picture on a light aircraft if nobody saw it take off or land.

I left my toast to get cold and went through into the old scullery. Pat and I had converted it into a store-cum-utility room and every few days I cleared the old papers and magazines out of the living-room and threw them in a corner there. The local council showed no interest in collecting them and about once a month I took the heap out to the yard and burned it. The last time had been more than a

fortnight ago and now the pile was over a foot high. I
started searching through the top papers for last Wednesday's.

Bridgeman was an art dealer. Graham had crashed on
Tuesday night and whatever had been in his plane, it must
have been pretty incriminating for Bridgeman to be so
anxious it shouldn't be found.

I was afraid I might have used the paper but it was still
there. I pulled it out, took it back to the kitchen and spread
it out on the table.

The report was brief, two short paragraphs at the foot of
an inside page. I read it through twice, tore it out and put it
in my back pocket. Then I went to phone Rekha Graham.

She answered almost at once.

"It's Clive Fordham," I told her. "Can I come to see
you?"

"What about? Has something happened?" Her tone was
guarded.

"Not exactly. I've found something I'd like to show you."

A moment's pause. Then she said, "When do you want to
come?"

"Would this morning be all right?"

"Very well." She didn't sound overjoyed at the prospect
of seeing me again. I couldn't blame her; I didn't like her
very much either.

"I'll be there in three quarters of an hour," I told her.

There wasn't time to clean the car but I decided I might
as well make myself reasonably presentable—the clothes I
wore round the house weren't that. I went upstairs and
changed into a fairly respectable shirt and trousers with
creases and no holes. Just in time, I remembered the report
in the pocket of the ones I had taken off.

There wasn't much traffic on the main road and I saw the
Jaguar follow me out of the lane two or three hundred

yards back. The lane led nowhere except to the village and a few farms and not many people used it as a short cut between main roads because there was a wider, less hilly way a mile nearer Stallford. I wondered who was likely to come that way who drove a Jaguar and couldn't think of anybody. Except one of the Bridgemans—and they didn't need to use the lane, there was no way to it from the house. Then I remembered the sunlight shining on something; had it been binoculars? If so, perhaps one of his men had been keeping watch from nearer the village this morning, waiting for me to leave.

Two miles farther on, the Jaguar was still there. I was doing fifty-five, fast enough on that winding stretch of road. I slowed to forty.

The gap between the two cars shortened momentarily, then widened again as the other driver realised I had slowed. I accelerated. The same thing happened, only this time in reverse.

A mile or so farther on the access road to the motorway turned off to the left. Opposite it a narrow lane led round two sides of a copse, then climbed a hill and meandered through a couple of villages before joining another main road. At the corner of the wood there was a gateway, the gate long since rotted away where a track led into it. And just before the wood the main road turned a sharp left-hand bend.

I drove slowly for the next three quarters of a mile, lulling the driver behind into a false sense of security. Then, into the bend and out of his sight, I jammed my foot hard on the accelerator. The Cortina surged forward. When I saw the turning on the right just ahead I turned the wheel sharply, hardly touching the brake pedal. Tyres screeching, the Ford lurched violently to the right. For a moment I thought it must turn over but then it steadied. Fortunately there was nothing coming in the other direction. I braked, turned in at the gateway and stopped. Five seconds later I saw the Jaguar flash past the end of the lane.

I knew I had only half a minute or so before the driver realised I was no longer in front of him and turned back. I reversed out of the wood and drove across the main road onto the motorway access road uncomfortably close to a Toyota that was heading north at a good seventy.

The Jaguar's driver would assume I had turned onto the M1 in the first place but there was no other junction for three or four miles and it would take him two or three minutes at least to find somewhere to turn and drive back. More with luck. The Cortina's speedometer registered seventy-eight.

At the next junction I left the motorway and took to by-roads. There was little traffic going into London and in spite of the time I had lost I still made it to the flat in under fifty minutes. The road outside Corhampton Court was deserted, no Sunday morning ritual of car cleaning here either. I parked the Cortina and ran up the stairs.

Today her sari was pale green. She was wearing a heavy necklace and the little diamond stars she always had in her ears. Even when she wore a shirt and jeans.

"Come in," she said, holding the door open for me.

I followed her into the big room. She limped slightly.

"How's your leg?" I asked.

"Much better, thank you."

It might be but still she found sitting down awkward. I sat on the chair facing her.

"What is it you want to show me?" she asked.

"Two things," I told her. "This first."

I handed her that morning's paper, folded so that she saw the story. She read it in silence.

"You think Derek was mixed up in that?" she asked when she had finished. Her voice was strangely expressionless.

"Isn't it possible?"

"Because I said he didn't mind very much if what he did was honest?"

"Partly. Not only that. He took off from that airfield just after five-thirty saying he was going to fly to Denham. He never landed there. It would only have taken him half an hour and he didn't crash until ten past nine; he must have been doing something all that time. That's why you went to the wood the other night, isn't it?"

"He wasn't a thief."

"Not when you knew him. People change. Especially when they start mixing with crooks."

"Are you a philosopher, Mr. Fordham?" Her tone was ironic.

"No more than most people. I'd like you to read this." I handed her the report I had torn from Wednesday's paper. Thieves had broken into the Old Manor House, Culcombe, Somerset, on Tuesday evening while the owner, Colonel Williamson, was out. They had tied up the two elderly servants and stolen two valuable paintings, a Courbet and a Stubbs. They had also taken a silver snuffbox.

"I didn't see this," Mrs. Graham said.

"It probably wasn't in the *Times*," I agreed. "That piece of canvas you found in the wood wasn't from a plane, was it?"

She shook her head. "It was from a picture. I could see that."

After all it was her job. But I hadn't. She had let me go on supposing it was from the plane because there hadn't been any point in telling me the truth. Or because she hadn't trusted me.

And I had thought she was keeping it because it came from the plane in which her husband had died.

Had she guessed the truth then? If so, what I was telling her wasn't news; she was prepared for it. I couldn't blame her if she fought against accepting it.

"Bridgeman didn't have time to save the paintings and he couldn't risk their being found in case they linked your husband with him," I said. "That's what you've been thinking too, isn't it?"

"No. I suppose I should have suspected something like that but I just thought Derek must have had a picture in the plane. I didn't think about its being stolen."

I believed her. "I went to a cocktail party at the Bridgemans' yesterday," I said.

For the first time since I came she smiled. "I wouldn't have thought you went to cocktail parties."

"I don't if I can help it. My brother was under the weather and I took his wife. She loves them and she wouldn't go alone."

"Oh." Somehow she made the single syllable very expressive.

"There was a friend of Bridgeman's there, an American named Lew Fucillo. Apparently he's a picture dealer in New York and he's over here on business."

"I've heard of him. He's not one of the better-known dealers."

"There was someone else, a very dark, smart girl."

"There's a lot of it about," Mrs. Graham agreed.

I grinned. "Bridgeman made a point of telling me Foskett surprised two poachers by the wood the other night. He thought they got away over my land. And I'm pretty sure he told Stephanie to find out if I'd picked up anything after the crash. She wasn't very subtle."

"She's not a very subtle girl."

"No."

"What did you tell her?"

"That I hadn't."

"That wasn't very honest of you, Mr. Fordham." She was laughing at me.

"Where's the snuffbox now?" I asked.

"I've still got it."

I wondered what she intended doing with it and hoped she would return it to Colonel Williamson. If it belonged to him; perhaps it wasn't the same one after all. She was watching me, a half-smile hovering round the corners of her mouth.

"I shall see it goes back to its owner," she assured me.

"We could take it," I suggested. The idea had only just occurred to me; I hadn't thought of it when I came. "Then we could ask the servants if they recognise your husband. Have you got a picture of him?"

She nodded. "Go now, you mean?"

Perhaps the prospect of driving all the way to Somerset and back with me didn't appeal to her. I was taking too much for granted. But still I wanted her to say she would. And I knew it wasn't only because of anything we might learn there.

"He was my husband," she reminded me quietly.

However much she might have come to dislike Graham, presumably she had loved him once. Now he was dead she wouldn't want his name blackened. And there was something else: any publicity was bound to involve her. I should have thought of that.

"I'm sorry," I told her awkwardly. Why did I behave so clumsily with her? I wondered.

"I don't think I could drive so far—my leg's still rather stiff." The spark of mischief was back in her eyes. "We could go if you drove. And we could take my car if you like."

It wasn't only the thought of driving the XJS that sent my spirits soaring.

"If it's all right with you," I said.

It took her only a few minutes to get ready. The clouds which had threatened rain earlier had blown away and it was another warm, sunny morning. I backed the Jaguar out of the line of cars and she climbed in.

She had to direct me through North London but once we reached the motorway I pressed my foot on the accelerator and the big car surged forward, sweeping majestically past the family saloons out for the day.

"You realise there may not be anybody there?" Mrs. Graham remarked suddenly. Neither of us had spoken for several minutes.

"No," I agreed.

"It's a long way to go for nothing."

"Farther than Hampstead for me."

"Yes."

"Would you rather we went back?"

"Certainly not, Mr. Fordham." She had a way of saying my name, a sort of mock formality, which suggested an intimacy I was sure she didn't intend.

"Somebody followed me this morning," I told her.

She turned her head. "Why?"

"I don't know. Presumably to see where I was going."

"Do you know who it was?"

"One of Bridgeman's men, I suppose. He has an XJ12 as well as his Rolls."

Mrs. Graham frowned. "How can you be sure whoever it was was following you?" she asked.

"I slowed and he slowed. When I accelerated, so did he. You don't get Jaguars along that stretch of road driving at thirty-five." I paused. "He followed me down the lane.

Their drive leads straight onto the main road; that means they were waiting for me. Watching me, I suppose."

"You don't like the idea?"

"No."

"What happened? Did he follow you right to the flat?"

"No, I lost him."

"How?"

I told her, trying not to sound too pleased with myself. She laughed.

"You've been watching too many films on television."

We stopped for petrol and coffee at the Membury service area. Mrs. Graham finished her coffee first and left me, saying she would see me at the car. But although I didn't hurry, when I reached it she wasn't there and she didn't reappear for several minutes.

At the A429 junction we left the motorway and turned south, then west. Culcombe, when we reached it, turned out to be a tiny village with a church, a pub, one shop and a cluster of old cottages.

"It's beautiful," Mrs. Graham commented. It was.

An elderly man outside one of the cottages told us the Old Manor was half a mile straight on. We drove along a lane that narrowed still more between high banks. It was very warm and through the open window the air was sweet with the scent of cow parsley.

We had gone more than half a mile when I saw a gravelled drive leading off to the left between twin rows of trees towards a house a quarter of a mile away. The drive badly needed resurfacing and in places there was more grass than gravel. The Jaguar bumped over potholes that were too close for me to avoid them.

I wondered where Graham had landed, then saw a level meadow on the right. The grass was cropped short and the trees would have hidden his plane from the house and helped to muffle its sound. It wouldn't have been too far to carry the pictures either.

The house was at least three hundred years old and not big enough to be imposing. A pleasant building with its weathered stone walls. But the flower beds were overgrown and there was an air of neglect about the place. I stopped the car and we got out.

"Have you brought the snuffbox?" I asked.

"No." My companion shook her head.

"I thought we were going to return it," I said, slightly irritated.

"I'll hand it to the police. They'll know what to do with it."

She was probably right. After all, it was possible the box hadn't been taken from here. Possible but hardly likely. That would have been too much of a coincidence.

"You've got the photograph?" I asked her.

"Yes. You'd better have it."

She took it out of her handbag and gave it to me. A picture of a man I had never seen. It came as a slight shock to realise I had had no idea what Graham looked like. It was a handsome face but the small mouth and the chin looked weak. Almost uncannily like the picture I had formed of him.

Mrs. Graham was watching me but she said nothing. I put the photograph in my wallet and rang the bell.

It was answered by an old man with a fringe of silver hair and a slight stoop. He looked harassed. I explained we would like to see Colonel Williamson if he was at home and he looked more disturbed than ever. But he showed us into a pleasant room overlooking the drive and said he would see if the Colonel was free.

While we waited I looked round. There wasn't much

furniture in the room and what there was was old and shabby.

Apparently the Colonel was free; he came bustling in almost at once. I disliked him on sight. He must have been in his middle sixties, a short, thickset man with a slack mouth, too clearly determined to impress us with his importance. A blotchy complexion and the watery eyes behind thick glasses suggested he drank too much.

Rekha Graham had walked across to look out of the window and he didn't see her for a moment. When he did I saw his expression change subtly. I tried to conceal my dislike and explained why we were there.

"Are you from the papers?" His tone was aggressive but there was caution behind it.

"Good God no!" Mrs. Graham said coolly.

I saw the hit had gone home and suppressed a grin. Her accent must have startled him; he looked uncomfortable.

"We're making some enquiries on behalf of my firm." She opened her bag and handed him one of her cards.

His eyes opened a little more. "Yes. Yes, I see," he muttered. It was amazing how quickly the bounce had gone out of him.

After that it was plain sailing. He rang for the servant who had admitted us and told him to fetch his wife, we would like to ask them one or two questions. The old boy went out again looking unhappy.

"I'll leave it to you, Mr. Fordham," Rekha said easily. She strolled out into the hall, pulling the door to behind her.

The Colonel watched her go but apparently decided he had better stay to hear what the old couple told me. I showed them the photograph of Graham and asked them if they had seen him before. The old man studied it for several seconds as if he couldn't make up his mind. Then he said it looked like one of the men who had tied them up and stolen the pictures but he couldn't be sure. His wife had no such inhibitions; she was certain.

There had been two of them. The other man had been about the same age but shorter and he spoke more roughly. Most of the time he had been behind them and she hadn't seen him very clearly. Her husband nodded agreement. They had rung the bell, overpowered the old man when he answered it and bundled him in here. Then they had told him to call his wife. When she came they had tied them both up and taken the pictures from the room across the hall. It was all over in a few minutes.

I guessed the experience had shaken them both pretty badly. The Colonel had found them still trussed up when he returned an hour later.

"Been to a friend's place," he explained. "If I'd been here they wouldn't have got away so easily."

I wondered who he was trying to convince. Probably himself.

"Did either of you hear an aeroplane about that time?" I asked the old couple.

They looked at each other and shook their heads.

"We were watching television in our room," the old man explained.

"Afterwards?" I suggested.

"No, sir."

They were probably too upset to notice and, anyway, from the intent way they had listened to my questions I suspected they were both slightly deaf.

Mrs. Graham came back. I thanked the couple and they went out.

"Well, thank you very much, Colonel," I said. "It's been very helpful."

He came to the door with us.

"They took a silver snuffbox too, didn't they?" I asked.

"Yes they did, the twisting bastards." It seemed to anger him more than the loss of the pictures. Maybe he had been more attached to it.

"Have you much silver, Colonel?" Mrs. Graham enquired politely.

He looked as if he'd like to tell her it was no bloody business of hers. Instead he answered curtly, "Not much."

"Has it rained here lately?" I asked him.

He looked surprised. "We had a shower yesterday morning. Nothing to speak of."

"What was it like on Tuesday?"

He thought for a minute. "Damned hot. Why? What's that got to do with it?"

"Nothing," I assured him blandly. "I was just curious. Had it rained much before then?"

"Not that I can remember. We haven't had any real rain for a fortnight."

"The police can't have found any tracks then." I opened the passenger side door for Mrs. Graham and hoped the Jaguar impressed him. I was glad we hadn't come in my car. "Thank you for your help, Colonel."

"A nasty little man," Rekha commented as I started the engine.

"Very," I agreed.

"Bloody wogs, don't you know?"

She looked at me. Her eyes were laughing and I laughed back.

The Colonel had gone back into the house. I drove a couple of hundred yards, stopped and looked in the rearview mirror. The house was hidden by a bend in the drive. Leaving the engine ticking over, I got out and climbed the low fence that bounded the meadow on the left. After a minute or two I found what I was looking for, the faint marks of tracks on the turf. I wondered if the police had noticed them. It didn't seem very likely; they wouldn't have had any reason to suspect a plane.

"What were you looking at?" Rekha asked when I returned to the car.

"Aeroplane tracks," I told her.

"Were there any?"

"Yes." The Jaguar moved forward smoothly.

"Did you notice anything about that room?"

"What about it?"

"The furniture was cheap. So it was in the other rooms. I looked. And the paintings were rubbish, there wasn't one that would have fetched fifty pounds in a sale."

Yet a few days ago a Stubbs and a Courbet had been stolen from that house. It was interesting but I couldn't see it was relevant.

"I think it might be a good idea to have a drink in the village," I said.

She looked at me but made no comment.

The pub had only just opened and the saloon was deserted when we entered it. From the desultory conversation we could hear, the public bar wasn't much busier. The landlady came through to serve us, a buxom, motherly-looking woman of about fifty with a startling mass of golden curls. Mrs. Graham said she would like a dry martini and I ordered a half of bitter for myself.

"That was a nasty business at the Old Manor the other night," I remarked while the landlady poured our drinks.

"Terrible," she agreed. "Poor old things."

"It must have been a shock for them. The Colonel too."

"Oh, him!" she said.

"He seemed rather an odd sort."

She pushed our glasses across the counter and I paid her. "We don't see much of him here."

"Has he lived there long?"

"It must be nearly thirty years now. He came when he married Miss Helen."

Publicans are usually pretty reticent about their customers—at least with strangers—but Williamson wasn't a customer and she didn't seem to mind talking about him. Trade was slack and she was prepared to chat. Rekha Graham and I listened.

It appeared the Colonel wasn't really a colonel at all. He had been a lieutenant in the Pay Corps. Then he was invalided out, got a commission in the Home Guard because of his time in the army and ended up a colonel. Miss Helen was the only child of the local squire and over forty when they married.

"Married her for her money," the landlady declared contemptuously. "Not that there was much of it by then. Shame it was, all the pictures and everything going. They say those two that was taken were the last ones he'd got. I reckon he could do with them now, with his tastes and the horses."

"Oh?" I said.

"It's a pity to see a nice old place like that going down, I always say." She looked suitably sad.

"It is," Rekha said.

"I expect the pictures were insured," I suggested.

"I expect so. But it's not the same, is it?"

"No," I agreed. All the same, I suspected Williamson would rather have the money than the paintings. He hadn't struck me as a man who would appreciate art.

A customer called from the other bar and the landlady went to serve him. Rekha and I finished our drinks and went out to the street.

NINE

It had been cool in the pub; out here the sun seemed to beat down more fiercely than ever. Culcombe dozed in the heat.

"Do you know the country round here?" Rekha asked.

"Only slightly; I've driven through."

"Let's explore then. There's no point in rushing back to London on a day like this." She gave me one of the direct, ironic looks I still found mildly disconcerting. "Unless you'd rather we did."

"No," I said. Considering I still wasn't sure I liked her the prospect was surprisingly attractive.

She got into the car and spread out a map, the Bartholomews 1:100,000 sheet of Reading and Salisbury Plain. Studying it together meant sitting very close. I could smell her perfume.

"That road looks as if it might be interesting," she suggested, tracing a narrow line with her finger.

"All right," I agreed.

It wandered through a succession of picturesque villages as sleepy as Culcombe. We drove slowly, enjoying the sunshine and the scenery. I almost forgot the crash and our reason for coming.

Just before one we found a pleasant old inn where they served lunches on Sundays. The dining room was small and low-ceilinged with genuine oak beams and spotless linen. Rekha ordered cold beef and a salad.

"You look surprised," she remarked when the waiter had gone.

"I'm sorry. I didn't think you'd eat beef."

She laughed. "I was brought up not to but I've lived in England since I was nineteen. Now if I want to, I do. It's not very often. I'm not a rebellious person; I've never seen the point in rebelling for the sake of it."

"Why did you come to England?" I asked her.

"I went up to Cambridge. My brother was at Magdalen and my father wanted me to have the same sort of education. It worried him terribly; he imagined me facing all sorts of moral dangers. I hadn't mixed with boys except my brother and cousins since I was thirteen and now I would be mixing with all those undergrads!"

"You've just one brother?"

"Yes, Ravi. You saw him when you came to the flat the other evening."

So that had been her brother. It was absurd to be so pleased—what difference did it make? Could it?

"He's a doctor." She smiled. "Because we're so far from home he feels he has to take my father's place. He worries about me too."

He needn't, I thought; she was quite capable of looking after herself. Then I remembered she had married Graham.

"Indian families are very close," she said. "I was a very happy little girl. Very protected. My father owns a block of flats and we all lived there, my mother, Ravi, my sisters and my uncles and aunts and cousins. All of us. We had a house in the country outside Bombay and one in the hills where we went for holidays."

"But you don't want to go back?"

"No. I go home every year and I enjoy seeing my family but life there seems very narrow and restricted after London. Perhaps I'll go back when I'm old; India's a wonderful country if you're old and have money."

"And if you're poor?" I asked.

She shrugged, her eyes solemn. "No, not then. How much land do you farm, Clive?"

It was the first time she had called me by my Christian name and it seemed a sign that subtly our relationship had changed. The idea was pleasant yet oddly disturbing.

"About four hundred acres," I told her.

"Is that a lot for where you are?"

"About average. A bit more, probably. But there are plenty of bigger farms."

"My father owns seven hundred acres." She said it without any hint of boasting. It was a fact and she thought I might be interested. "He has a factory in Bombay; he just owns the land and the tenants farm it. They grow rice and coconuts and pay him two thirds of everything."

"Really?"

"It's usual."

I remembered hearing that India's was still basically a village economy. Or was that only what Ghandi had wanted? I wasn't sure and felt slightly guilty that I knew so little about it. About everywhere, except a small corner of England.

"Where did you meet your husband?" I asked her.

"At a sale. Three years ago. I suppose he thought it would be amusing to have an Indian girlfriend. Trendy— you know?" The mischievous look was back in her eyes but now she was mocking herself. "Especially one with a rich father."

"When did you find that out?"

"Too late." She hesitated. "How long were you married?"

"Four years." Usually I disliked people asking me about

Pat; our relationship had been too private. Now for some reason I wanted to talk about her. "We were very happy."

"Yes, I guessed you were."

"How?"

"The way you look when you mention her. It's guarded. And you shy away, as if you want to keep her to yourself."

I didn't know what to say. Rekha Graham saw too much.

The waiter brought our food, then the bottle of Moselle I had ordered. For a minute or two neither of us spoke. Then I said, "There are two outbuildings behind Bridgeman's garage. One of them has been done up and the window blocked in. There's a new door with a Yale lock too. I'd like to know what he keeps there."

"It doesn't sound the sort of place he'd store valuable paintings," Rekha commented.

"Not for long, no," I agreed. "I wonder how he gets them out of the country."

That, I was pretty sure, was the secret of the whole business.

Neither of us wanted a pudding; we had coffee, I paid the bill and we went out to the car park. A small boy who had been admiring the Jaguar saw us coming and retreated a few feet. Rekha smiled at him and he grinned back shyly.

"Would you rather drive now?" I asked her.

"Not unless you want me to."

I didn't. After all, I might never have another chance to drive an XJS.

It was five o'clock before we got back to Corhampton Court; we had driven through the lanes and only taken to the motorway when we were past Reading. Now there was a dirty Ford Granada standing next to my Cortina. I manoeuvred the Jaguar past it and parked.

"I owe you for the petrol," I said. We had driven nearly

two hundred and fifty miles and at sixteen miles to the gallon that was a lot of petrol.

"And I owe you for lunch," Rekha returned lightly. "And a drink at Culcombe."

"It was my idea we went."

"And mine we came a long way back."

Stalemate.

"All right," I agreed.

She opened the door on her side. "You're coming up, aren't you?" She sounded as if she wanted me to.

I locked the car, walked over to where she was waiting and handed her the keys. The Cortina looked out of place. Like me, I thought. It had a dent in the rear bumper where Tom had backed a tractor into it. That was several months ago but I hadn't got round to doing anything about it. The car ran just as well dented as before.

"One of these days I'll get a new car," I remarked.

"Why?" Rekha asked. "If it does what you want?"

Because I didn't like the inferiority complex it gave me. The Jaguar was exciting to drive but it was a reminder of the gap between us and I didn't want to be reminded. Not any longer.

I followed her through the swing doors and up the stairs. It was very quiet. I supposed that when you rented one of those flats you paid for plenty of soundproofing. On the landing she stopped, fished her key out of her bag and pushed it into the lock.

The hall looked just as it had done when we left this morning. The little console table was standing against the wall with the Indian drawing over it, the living-room door slightly ajar. I noticed that Rekha was limping again; her leg must have stiffened after sitting in the car so long. She pushed the door open wider. Then, half into the room, she stopped dead.

I heard the quick intake of breath and a muttered oath, so quiet I almost missed it. Then she went in. I followed.

The room was a shambles. The furniture had been overturned and drawers pulled out, their contents scattered on the floor. The pictures had been torn from the walls. In the dining area the sideboard cupboards were emptied.

So much I took in before Rekha turned and I saw the horror leap into her eyes.

"Clive!" she gasped.

I started to turn too. Two men were standing behind the door. One was Foskett, the other, younger and thicker-set, I didn't know. He was clutching a heavy glass vase. I saw him raise it and ducked. A fraction of a second too late. The vase crashed on my left shoulder with a force that sent a wave of pain shooting through it. I tried to raise my arm and couldn't.

Hell! I thought. If my shoulder was broken that was it. Sweat stood out on my forehead.

Matey was coming forward. I swung a right at his head. It caught him too high to do any damage but he staggered momentarily. Out of the corner of my eye I saw Foskett aiming a blow and lunged towards him, bringing my right knee up hard. It was no time for niceties and my left arm was useless. The blow landed well below belt level. He grunted with pain and went backwards.

After that everything was confused. I heard Rekha gasp but there wasn't time to look round, Foskett was coming for me again. He was tough and he knew more about fighting dirty than I did. Fortunately for me, he hadn't room to use his feet.

I felt his hands groping for my throat and sank my knee into his belly again. He staggered slightly and for a moment I thought I had the upper hand. If Rekha could keep his friend occupied while I dealt with him . . .

My confidence was short-lived. As I went forward my foot caught one of the overturned chairs and I fell to my knees. It was all Foskett needed. Before I could regain my feet he was on me.

I could see the fury in his eyes. Maybe using my knee hadn't been such a good idea. I tried to push him off but with only one good arm I was virtually helpless. I saw him start to swing his right foot viciously and managed to sway out of the way. Just in time. I grabbed his ankle and pulled. He staggered and grabbed at the chair.

"No!" Rekha cried behind me.

The next second something hard struck my left side just below my ribs. Matey's boot.

God! I thought. I felt sick.

My brain said I'd got to do something.

Couldn't. Couldn't bloody well move.

The next time it wasn't my body; he kicked my head. I felt the terrible jarring impact, then the lights went out.

Consciousness returned slowly. A gradually growing awareness of pain. Uncomfortable at first. Very soon much worse. I retched. My head was throbbing violently. It felt as if somebody was pounding it with a red-hot hammer. My whole body seemed to be on fire. There was a sharp pain in my side and my shoulder ached abominably. But I could move my arm so it wasn't broken.

I felt something wet on my forehead and realised Rekha was squatting beside me bathing it with a damp cloth.

"That's nice," I murmured.

I had lost my glasses and I must have looked pretty silly lying there but it was a long time since a woman had fussed over me.

"Clive, are you all right?"

Her anxiety made me feel a bit better. It was a pity it didn't do anything to ease the pain.

"More or less," I answered. "What about you?"

"They didn't hit me."

Just pushed her around, I thought. I was thankful it wasn't anything worse.

I tried to sit up. A mistake. For one thing, it made my head ache more. It didn't do my side much good either.

"You look very young and defenceless without your glasses," Rekha said.

"I feel defenceless."

It was the understatement of the week, I felt a wreck. Must look one too.

She leaned forward and kissed me on the cheek. I was too taken aback to respond. Even if I could have moved. Then she stood up.

"Here are your glasses," she said.

By some freak of good fortune they weren't broken. I put them on.

"Now I'm going to call a doctor."

"No," I told her.

"Why not?"

"Because it would mean a lot of questions. He'd probably tell the police."

She thought for a moment, eyeing me anxiously. "I'll get Ravi."

I couldn't argue about that. I knew I ought to let a doctor look at me.

"All right," I agreed.

What was below your ribs? Spleen? I had no idea. Only that whatever it was hurt like hell and I hoped it wasn't bleeding inside. That seemed only too possible.

But at least I could see all right. No double vision.

"Can you give me a hand up?" I asked her.

It took all her strength and a ridiculous amount of will-power on my part but I felt better on my feet. Something to do with morale, I supposed.

While she went out to the hall to phone her brother I managed to make it to the window and look out. There was an empty space beside my Cortina. The Granada had gone.

I stood there, leaning on the window sill and hoping the pain would ease enough to let me get back to one of the chairs, Rekha had turned them the right way up again but the settee was still lying on its back.

"He's coming straight over," she said, coming back into the room.

I made it to the chair and while we waited for him she set about clearing up the mess. Apart from the vase, nothing appeared to have been broken.

"There doesn't seem to be anything missing," she said. "And they didn't go in the other rooms."

We had probably returned before they had finished in here. I wondered what would have happened if she had been alone when they came.

"Where's the snuffbox?" I asked.

"It isn't here."

"You said you had it."

"It's in the safe at my office. You think that's what they were after?"

It couldn't be anything else, they weren't ordinary house-breakers. Bridgeman must have read in the paper about its being stolen. Perhaps he already knew about Graham's lit-tle ways. And he knew he must still have had it with him when the plane crashed. The fire wouldn't have destroyed it and he couldn't risk its being found. If it was, the police would start asking awkward questions, the plane would be linked with the theft and he might become involved.

"Why should they come here looking for it?" Rekha asked.

I told her what I believed.

"That would be like Derek." Her voice was flat but there was an undertone of bitterness. "If he was there to steal the pictures and saw it he wouldn't be able to resist taking it. I didn't know he'd gone so far."

"Are you going to call the police when I've gone?" I asked her.

She looked round the room. "There isn't much point now, is there?"

The doorbell rang and she went to answer it. When she came back her brother was with her. He eyed me coolly. His eyes were like Rekha's, dark and expressionless. All the same, I had the feeling he didn't like me.

"My sister says you've had an accident," he said. "What happened?"

Rekha had left it to me to tell him as much as I wanted.

"Two men took a dislike to me," I said.

He didn't show any sign of curiosity. Perhaps he had to attend to muggers' victims every day.

"Take off your shirt, please."

I obeyed. It wasn't easy using only one arm and he helped me. Rekha had gone through to the kitchen and closed the door.

He explored my side with light, cool fingers, not saying anything. Then my skull. Finally he shone a tiny light in my eyes and examined them.

"You must be X-rayed," he said when he had finished.

I nodded. I had expected that.

"You will have to go to the hospital. I will take you in my car."

He went to have a word with his sister, then to phone the

hospital. Rekha came back into the room looking concerned.

"What did he say?" I asked her.

"Nothing. Just that he can't tell until he's seen the X-rays. He's a good doctor."

When he returned she told him she would take me to the hospital; her car would be more comfortable than his. I could see he didn't like the idea much.

"Very well," he agreed.

We went out together. We seemed to be spending a lot of time driving each other to hospitals.

TEN

We were there a long time. At last Ravi came and told me I
was lucky, Matey's boot hadn't caused any serious damage.
I had escaped with nothing worse than some pretty severe
bruising and a few cuts. Unpleasant but not dangerous.

"You should be able to go home tomorrow, Mr. Fordham," he said.

Tomorrow? I had no intention of spending the night
here. I told him so as politely as I could.

He didn't try to hide his disapproval but if I insisted on
going there wasn't much he could do about it. Apart from
making it clear he thought I was a fool and he was washing
his hands of me.

"How will you get home?" he wanted to know.

"I'll drive."

"It won't be very comfortable."

"I'll manage."

He shrugged and helped me dress again, then we went
out to where Rekha was waiting.

"His skull is not fractured," Ravi told her. "The blow
must have been a glancing one. There is some severe bruising but no internal injury."

"How long will he have to stay here?" she asked.

"I'm going home now," I told her.

"Is that wise?"

She looked at Ravi. No response there, he just shrugged
again.

"If you mean to go, I'll drive you," she said.

"No."

"You can fetch your car another time."

Ravi looked more disapproving than ever.

"What about your leg?" I asked her.

"It's better now."

"You were limping this afternoon."

"What about your leg?" Ravi demanded.

"Nothing." She looked annoyed and I realised she hadn't told him.

There was an awkward little silence. Rekha walked to the door.

"I'm very grateful," I told Ravi.

He didn't answer, just nodded. Then he called, "I will ring you later, Rekha."

"There's no need," she told him coldly, "but you can if you like. Goodbye, Ravi."

It was cooler outside. I could walk all right and the pain wasn't so bad now. Perhaps it was knowing there was nothing seriously wrong. Or just that the first shock had passed. Nevertheless, it was bad enough to be going on with.

Rekha turned the Jaguar and drove out of the yard into the street. I glanced at the clock and was surprised to see it was still not quite nine o'clock.

She handled the car well, not taking risks but not dawdling either. We had almost reached the North Circular when she said suddenly, "I'm sorry about Ravi."

"What about him?" I asked.

She looked sideways at me. "If you don't know, it doesn't matter."

"I know he doesn't like me."

"It's not you. Ravi's not a fool, he wouldn't make up his mind about a person so quickly."

I reflected that she and I had both disliked Williamson on sight.

"He has very fixed ideas," Rekha said. "He saw you leaving my flat the other evening, now he finds us there together. I told you, he feels responsible for me."

"You mean he doesn't like my seeing you? Because I'm English?" That was a novel idea to me and I could see the irony of it. But it didn't stop me being angry.

"Derek was English," Rekha said.

I grinned. That seemed more sensible than showing my anger. "I hope he doesn't judge us all by Derek."

"He was very upset when we were married. He never liked Derek. He wasn't exactly glad when he was proved right but now he's afraid . . ." She stopped abruptly.

"Afraid of what?" I wanted to hear her say it.

She hesitated, choosing her words. "That I might become involved with an Englishman again. He's more aware than I am of the differences in attitudes."

She concentrated on the road and we didn't talk much for some time. I wondered what she was thinking.

The sun had set by the time she turned off up the lane and it was almost dark. She took the track to the house slowly, out of consideration for me or the Jaguar's springs, and stopped.

"Will Ravi phone?" I asked.

"I expect so. He'll want to be sure I've got back all right."

"Thank you for bringing me."

"Thank you for today; I enjoyed it." She leaned across and kissed me. On the mouth this time. I put my arm round her and for a moment she yielded. Then she sighed and drew away.

"I must go."

"Yes," I agreed.

"Good night, Clive."

"Good night."

I climbed out and watched while she reversed the car. When the lights disappeared round the corner I turned and walked across to the back door.

They hadn't bothered to look for the key, just forced a jemmy in the side of the door and levered it open. The wood was splintered. I swore, guessing what I would find. Why hadn't Brandy driven them off?

I soon saw why. He was lying on his side on the kitchen floor. There was a small wound in his head just above his left eye and when I touched him he was stiff. He had a piece of cloth clenched between his teeth but at least there wasn't much blood.

A farmer can't afford to be sentimental about animals but I felt like crying. I had had Brandy since he was six weeks old. His mother had belonged to Elizabeth and Peter and they had given him to me for a birthday present soon after Pat died. I carried him out to one of the barns and laid him on the straw; it was too late to bury him tonight.

Back in the house the rooms were in the same state as Rekha's living-room. Only here they hadn't been disturbed and they had gone right through the house. My side still hurt pretty badly and my head ached; clearing up the mess would have to wait until the morning. I went upstairs, undressed as best I could and fell into bed.

Monday started bright. I had taken two pills Ravi had given me and I woke feeling heavy and listless but a good deal better than last night. My head was clearer and in place of the pain my side ached dully. I got up, carried Brandy to the top field and buried him there before Fred and Tom arrived. They would miss him sooner or later but I didn't feel up to inventing explanations for his absence just yet.

The barley was almost ready for combining. As I walked

back down the hill something on Bridgeman's land caught my eye; the sun was shining on some bright object. Then I realised what it was, somebody near the corner of the wood was using binoculars. Watching me. Hell! I thought. But there was nothing amusing about it.

Tom was propping up his motorbike in the yard. He gave the spade I was carrying a curious look but he didn't say anything.

Fred arrived a few minutes later. We talked about one of the bullocks he thought was in poor shape, then I took Tom to look at the drier in the big barn. If there wasn't much rain in the next day or two we should be able to start the harvest this week and I didn't want that letting me down.

But my mind wasn't on what we were doing. Two days ago I had resolved that whatever Bridgeman might be up to and whatever part Graham had played in it, it was no concern of mine. If he was crooked, that was up to the police. I had a farm to run and a living to make and I had better concentrate on it.

It made good sense.

But that was two days ago and yesterday had changed things. I was involved now whether I liked it or not. When Rekha and I disturbed Foskett and his pal in her flat they could have laid me out easily enough if all they wanted was to get away. There had been a calculated viciousness about the way Matey had put in the boot. And their shooting Brandy.

As if they had been intended as a warning.

Something else bothered me: the bullet that killed Brandy hadn't come from a shotgun. I was no firearms expert but I knew enough to see that. The wound had been caused by a large-calibre bullet. That meant it had been fired from a revolver or a pistol of some sort.

If I was right, after the paintings were stolen they were

flown to Langley Farm. That was safer than taking them by road; the police couldn't set up road-blocks in the sky and there was always a chance somebody might notice a car or van near a house at the time of the robbery and remember it later. No one would take much notice of a light plane flying over and if they did, it would be almost impossible to track it. Unless it crashed. Besides which it was quicker and speed meant safety. Within an hour or two of the theft the pictures would be at the farm, locked away in the shed behind the garage.

But what happened then? I still had no idea how they were smuggled out of the country.

Bridgeman's gallery must play some part in the scheme, but what? He could hardly have paintings worth hundreds of thousands of pounds lying about there to be seen. Come to that, how were pictures sent abroad in the ordinary way? I knew the exporters needed licences if they were really valuable, but that was about all I did know. I would have to ask Rekha. I must ring her anyway, to arrange about collecting my car.

When I went into the house for some coffee I phoned her office. The telephonist sounded young and superior.

"Mrs. Graham, please," I told her.

"Just a moment."

There was a brief pause, then another woman's voice said, "Can I help you?" Not Rekha.

"Mrs. Graham, please," I repeated.

"I'm her secretary. May I ask what it's in connection with?"

"A personal matter," I told her. "Stolen pictures, two poachers and a snuffbox."

"*What?*" She wasn't sure if I was pulling her leg or just mad but at least she sounded more human.

"She'll understand," I said.

"Oh. Who shall I tell her is calling?"

"The other poacher. But don't you think she'll know?"

"Yes, I suppose she will," the secretary conceded, her manner slipping a little more. "Will you hold on?"

I imagined her explaining to Rekha, not knowing whether to laugh or be indignant. Maybe Rekha wouldn't be amused. I wished I hadn't played the fool.

There was a click and she said, "I take it the other poacher's feeling better."

"Yes," I admitted. "I'm mad."

"Mad angry or mad peculiar?"

"Both probably. I meant angry. They were here yesterday, the whole house is like your living-room. And they shot Brandy."

"Oh no! You mean they killed him?"

"Yes." I was glad she sounded so distressed. "He must have gone for them; he had a piece of cloth in his teeth."

"I'm sorry, Clive." No effusions, but I knew she meant it.

"Yes," I said. "How do you send paintings abroad?"

"By air usually."

"But how? When do you need a licence?"

"When the sale value of a picture is more than four thousand pounds."

"It's as simple as that?"

"Yes, basically. You need the proper documentation, of course." She paused. "Your friend wouldn't be able to get licences for those pictures."

Obviously. Not when he had stolen them.

"It would be pretty risky sending them out in the usual way, I should think," Rekha went on. "After all those thefts the Customs might open the cases."

That was what was puzzling me. Bridgeman had been so careful in everything else.

"They get them out somehow," I said.

"When are you coming for your car?"

"Can I collect it today? There's somewhere I want to go."

"Yes, of course. But you aren't going to take any chances, are you?"

"No," I promised, glad she was interested.

We said goodbye and I replaced the phone. Then I picked it up again and dialled another London number. Bill Mackay was the deputy news editor on one of the national dailies, a Scot from a village near Edinburgh. He drove up to town from the village every day in an elderly, battered Morris 1800. We played tennis once or twice a week during the summer and met at the Fox for a drink before lunch most Saturdays. Last year he had decided he wanted to keep goats. Heaven knew why—it seemed a strange ambition to me. I found two for him and now he claimed proudly that he and his family produced all the milk and cheese they needed and soon they were going to start making their own butter. I suspected his wife Valerie did most of the work but I had to admit he was serious about it.

"You know these art thefts there have been from country houses," I said when we had exchanged the usual pleasantries.

"Yes?" He sounded surprised.

"Could you find out the dates and places?"

"What on earth for? Are you setting up as a private eye or something?"

"It was just something I was reading. It's given me an idea," I told him. That was true at least.

"I suppose so. When do you want to know?"

"As soon as possible."

"Okay. Leave it with me just now. It'll take an hour or so."

"Thanks, Bill," I said.

While I waited for him to ring back I started putting the house to rights. It was such a shambles I hardly knew where to start but I decided that as I spent most of my time in the kitchen and living-room I'd do best to tackle them first. They were more or less restored to normal when the phone rang.

It was Bill. There had been five thefts that appeared to be the work of the same gang, spread over the last five months. Sometimes two or three weeks between them, sometimes longer. I found a piece of paper and a ballpoint pen and he read out a list of dates and places. They were all private houses or properties belonging to trusts; there were no museums or art galleries. Those were too likely to be protected by guards and alarm systems, I guessed. Private people didn't always bother or, if they did, the systems were old and easily put out of action.

"That's the lot," he said.

"Thanks," I told him. "You've been a great help."

"You're not going in for the same game, are you?" he asked.

"I wouldn't know how to get rid of the stuff."

"They tell me that's the hardest part," he agreed.

No help there. I said goodbye and went to find a map of Berkshire. It was just over forty miles from Rekha's flat to the airfield where Graham had hired the Cherokee. Tom took me to Stallford station on the back of his motorbike. I didn't have a crash helmet but we saw no policemen.

The airfield was miles from anywhere. You approached it along a narrow by-road, rounded a bend and there was the clubhouse. It was little more than a big shed with one or two smaller buildings near it and a large hangar. Cloud had built up since I left the farm and a windsock hung limp in

the rain that was falling. Not a sight to raise the spirits. Even
the two little planes parked near the hangar looked forlorn.

I drove across loose gravel and stopped as close to the
clubhouse entrance as I could get. The place was hardly a
hive of activity, I couldn't see a soul. Inside there was a
large room with a few easy chairs, others made of metal and
ugly orange plastic, some card tables and a bar. The grille
was down. I saw a door marked OFFICE and tapped on it.

The man who called "Come in" was small, wiry and
about forty-five. I had seen him before, at the inquest. His
desk, with another chair, a steel cupboard and a filing cabi-
net, occupied most of the floor space. I eyed the calendar
on the wall; it had a photograph of a well-developed blonde
wearing a coy smile and little else, and an advertisement for
a tyre dealer.

"Morning. Can I help you?" The manager sounded busi-
nesslike.

"I'm not sure," I admitted. "One of your planes crashed
near Stallford last week."

You could almost see him withdraw into himself. Too
many questions had probably put him on guard. He wasn't
ready for any more.

"What about it?" he demanded.

"I'm acting for Mrs. Graham, the pilot's widow. I wonder
if you could tell me the dates when he flew from here
during the last six months. Say from the beginning of February."

He didn't like it. Perhaps he suspected I was a lawyer, or
represented an insurance company. Either way it could
mean difficulties and he didn't want them.

"There was nothing wrong with that plane when it took
off," he said.

"Did anybody suggest there was?" I asked him.

"No."

"You needn't worry, I've nothing to do with insurance or anything like that, this is a personal thing. Mrs. Graham would like to know."

He looked slightly mollified but still I could see him turning over the possibilities in his mind. He probably remembered Rekha's saying at the inquest that she and Graham had separated a year ago; why should she want to know?

"Who are you?" he demanded.

"My name's Fordham; I'm just a friend of Mrs. Graham's. You can ring her to check if—"

He shook his head. It was probably his inclination to be helpful when he could and besides, he knew that if he refused it might look as if he had something to hide. He decided to take a chance.

"All right," he agreed. "I don't see why not. But you'll have to give me a few minutes."

He went out, closing the door behind him. I walked across to the window and looked out. Rain was dripping from a break in the gutter, forming a puddle on the gravel. A car went past on the road, sending up a spray of dirty water.

The manager was gone nearly ten minutes. I had exhausted the charms of the view and the girl on the calendar and returned to my chair by the time he returned.

"Here you are," he said, handing me a sheet of paper on which he had jotted down a list of dates and places. "I've put down the airfields he flew to as well in case you wanted to know."

I thanked him and put the list away in my wallet.

"It didn't have anything to do with the crash," the manager said, "but he was always having trouble with his radio. Just one of those things; nobody else did. On four of those flights there he reported it went out of action after he had taken off. Blew a fuse or something."

"That's a pretty high proportion, isn't it?" I suggested.

"Very." He looked mildly disturbed.

"So you lost contact with him? You wouldn't know where he was going?"

"No."

"I'm not suggesting anything," I said, "but could he have put it out of action deliberately?"

"Yes, he could." The manager looked more disturbed than ever. "It happens."

He walked to the door with me. "I've been here six years and that was the first fatal accident we've had," he remarked.

I nodded, thanked him again and walked back across the clubroom and out into the drizzle. In the car I took out his list and the one Bill Mackay had dictated and compared them. Graham had hired a plane on a dozen occasions since the middle of February; on five of those days there had been a robbery. To put it another way, every time a valuable painting had been stolen during that period he had been flying.

I started the car and headed back towards London. It might not be conclusive but it was good enough for me.

ELEVEN

My most direct route home entailed leaving the motorway at Slough East. I saw the half-mile sign and moved across into the nearside lane ready for the turn. Then I remembered that Rekha had said Bridgeman's gallery was just off Bond Street and I drove straight on. I might as well go and have a look at it while I was out; I wouldn't get any more work done today.

I parked the car and went in search of a telephone box to look up the address. When I found one there was no directory. I could have rung the exchange and asked them but I thought it wouldn't take me long to find it myself.

I was wrong. Unlike supermarkets and garages, art galleries maintain decently discreet fronts. You don't see their names in neon lights. I had been along one side of the street, exploring every side turning, and was halfway back along the other when I realised that Bridgeman might call it the Plantagenet or something equally unlikely. His name probably didn't appear at all.

It was raining more heavily now and I was wet and fed up. For some reason rain is always more unpleasant in towns than in the country. One is less likely to be sensibly dressed and it drips heavily from buildings as you dodge the umbrellas. Passing traffic splashes your legs. I was on the point of saying to hell with it and going home.

Then, down a narrow side street, I found it. A large window displaying a single, rather sombre landscape with

"The Bridgeman Gallery" in ornate gilt lettering over it. I walked past and studied it across the street from a safe distance.

Now that I was here I hadn't any idea what I was going to do. Bridgeman was probably there; I could hardly walk in and tell him brightly, "I was just passing and I thought I'd come in and have a look round to see if you've any stolen pictures here." We weren't on those terms. I should have left it until lunchtime tomorrow, then I could have waited for him to emerge. But I hadn't.

I looked away along the street and nearly missed him. He came out, turned right without looking in my direction and walked off towards Bond Street. Hoping he wasn't merely going round the corner for twenty cigarettes, I waited until he had reached it, then crossed the street and walked back to the gallery.

It consisted of two smallish rooms linked by an arch with an office at the back. Both rooms were deserted. I wandered round, looking at the pictures. They were old—apparently Bridgeman didn't deal in modern art—and mostly landscapes with two or three portraits and a single still life. I turned away from a portrait of a couple in eighteenth-century dress and found myself facing an Impressionist painting of a river scene. The picture Eunice Bridgeman had painted that hung in their drawing-room was a copy; I was looking at the original.

The gallery had a hushed air that seemed to have nothing to do with there being nobody else about. I suspected that conversations were conducted in whispers, as if it were a church. Perhaps it was the oppressive effect of the prices.

The door was open and I could hear a voice raised angrily in the office. An American's voice. Fucillo's. Then he moved and I saw his stocky figure, his head thrust forward. There was no reason why I should be surprised—after all,

he had told me he often bought paintings from Bridgeman
—but finding him here was a shock.

"You're not getting another cent," he snarled. The ve-
neer of charm had gone.

"Graham promised me twenty thousand." It was a man's
voice, complaining. I was sure I had heard it before but
couldn't remember where.

"No more," Fucillo grated.

I told myself I should have guessed he was involved.
Rekha's knowing of him had misled me, but Bridgeman had
a legitimate business too. The police were convinced the
stolen paintings were sold abroad; was that Fucillo's role in
the organisation?

Knowing he was mixed up in it didn't make me feel any
happier. It looked as if I had walked into a bigger hornets'
nest than I had suspected.

A woman came out of the office and closed the door
behind her. She was about thirty, very dark and slim, her
beauty set off by the simplicity of her dress. I had seen her
before, talking to Bridgeman at the party. And later, watching me looking at the outbuilding. Seeing her was another
shock.

I thought she must have seen me but she made for a desk
at one side of the inner room. Then she noticed me and
stopped. I waited for some sign of recognition. If she
shouted for the American all I had to do was walk out; once
I was in the street there was nothing they could do. For the
time being; I had to go home sometime. I remembered
Brandy and cold fingers seemed to touch my spine.

But if she had recognised me she wasn't going to let it
show. She switched on a professional smile, welcoming but
empty.

"Good afternoon, sir. Can I help you?" She had a cool
up-market voice.

"I was just looking round," I said. "That's all right, isn't it?"

"Oh yes of course, sir."

With Fucillo ranting like an angry bull in the office? She must be joking. But she could hardly ask me to leave. She smiled again. It was a minor achievement; by four o'clock on a muggy day like this most women were beginning to fray round the edges, but she looked as if she had just stepped out of a beautician's. Her eyes took in my shabby jacket and trousers; I hadn't bothered to change to go to the flying club. Perhaps that was why she hadn't recognised me at first.

I could see she had now by the way she half screwed up her eyes and frowned slightly. She turned on her heel and started back towards the office, half running. I decided that if she was going to fetch Fucillo, discretion was the better part of valour.

But when she was still several feet short of it the office door opened and I heard a man's footsteps coming towards me. I couldn't see him from where I was standing behind the arch and I wanted to know who it was Graham had promised twenty thousand pounds. I ducked back into the nearest corner and a second or two later a man came hurrying through. It was Williamson.

Shock number three. I told myself I should have recognised his voice but I hadn't been prepared to find him here.

He passed without looking at me, pulled open the street door and blundered out. Through the glass I saw him turn right, in the direction of Bond Street.

Behind me Fucillo exclaimed, "Goddamn little punk, trying to twist us for another ten thousand!" In a calmer tone he added, "Harry's got to get that picture, Kay, it's worth a hell of a lot to us."

"He will," the girl said quickly. "Lew?"

"Yeah?"

She must have whispered something to him; I couldn't hear it. Nevertheless, I had a pretty good idea what it was about. I started across the outer room after Williamson. Apart from any other considerations, the sooner I talked to him the better.

"Here?" the American demanded.

Footsteps crossed the wood floor.

"No!" Kay told him. "Put that away, Lew. Not here."

I looked back over my shoulder. Fucillo was holding a gun in his right hand. It was pointing straight at my heart.

"Stop!" he growled.

I was only three feet from the door. I didn't fancy my chances if I did as he said; they might be better if I kept going. Through the glass pane in the door I could see a woman just outside. Her hand was reaching for the handle. A woman in a sari. What was Rekha doing here?

I pulled the door open, blocking her way. If once she entered the gallery she might be in danger.

"Rekha!" I exclaimed in an undertone.

Her eyes met mine and I was shocked by their blank expression. She might never have seen me before.

I had to step aside then and she walked past me as if I hadn't existed. I looked round. Fucillo's right hand was in his jacket pocket.

"Why, hallo there," he said, smiling.

"Hallo." Rekha answered him as if he were an old friend.

I stepped out into the wet street shaken and bewildered. What was going on? But there was no time to think about anything else now, Williamson had almost a minute's start. I began running towards the corner.

Despite the rain, Bond Street was crowded with shoppers and tourists. I looked right, then left. There was no sign of Williamson's stocky figure with its strutting walk. If he was going far he would almost certainly take a taxi or the tube. I reckoned the tube was the better bet and turned right.

It took me another minute to spot him. He was walking more slowly now, near the edge of the pavement. People jostled him but he seemed oblivious of them. Keeping close to the shop fronts on the right, I quickened my pace. Just as I came abreast of him a woman clutching an umbrella and several parcels dropped one of them. She stopped dead and stooped to pick it up and I bumped into her.

"Say!" she exclaimed in an accent as marked as Fucillo's.

"Sorry," I apologised.

"That's okay. I guess it was my fault."

I picked up the parcel and handed it to her, glancing across to see if Williamson was looking. He wasn't; he was already several yards farther on. The woman smiled her thanks. I grinned back and hurried on. Fifty yards past Williamson I turned and sauntered back. He didn't see me until the last moment and we almost collided.

"Colonel Williamson!" I exclaimed. "It is Colonel Williamson, isn't it?"

His protuberant little eyes peered at me through his thick glasses. He didn't remember me. Perhaps he was too disturbed, remembering what had happened at the gallery.

"I came to see you yesterday about your robbery," I reminded him. "With Mrs. Graham."

"Uh," he grunted. The memory didn't seem to have done anything to cheer him. From my point of view, I thought, that might be a good thing. If he was frightened he might be more easily persuaded to talk.

"Fancy meeting you here," I observed chattily. "Do you often come up to London?"

"No."

He made a move to pass me but I stepped in his way. It was only then I remembered I was wearing my shabby old clothes, hardly suitable gear for an executive of a famous auction house. It was time to put the pressure on before he started wondering.

"You didn't get much change out of them at the gallery, did you?" I said.

He succeeded in looking angry and frightened at the same time. Like a rat caught in a trap. Only this rat had made his own cage and walked straight in.

"What do you mean?" he demanded.

"Fucillo wasn't very sympathetic, was he?"

"I don't know what you mean." He studied me furtively, clearly wondering how much I knew.

"The American," I told him. "Didn't you know his name? He's a friend of Bridgeman's. I don't suppose Bridgeman was any more helpful, was he?"

Pedestrians pushed past us on one side, traffic on the other. People tried to avoid the spray thrown up by cars and taxis, muttering as they had to go round us.

"I've never heard of Bridgeman," Williamson mumbled.

"Just as you like," I agreed. I knew he was playing for time while he thought up some story to explain what I had overheard at the gallery. But I knew too much. Guessed a good deal more.

A taxi was coming towards us with its flag up. I waved to the driver, grasped Williamson's arm and propelled him towards it. He resisted feebly.

"Fucillo's just behind," I said softly.

He looked over his shoulder and I saw the fear return to his eyes. Christ! I thought. Was the American really there? But if he was, what could he do here in the middle of a crowded street?

"It's not Fucillo," Williamson said.

I started breathing normally again. The taxi had stopped.

I didn't have to push Williamson, he almost tripped in his anxiety to get in.

"Paddington," I told the driver.

"Right, sir."

I followed Williamson into the back and sat down on the folding seat facing him. It had been a lie about Fucillo following us but his nerves were in such a state he was willing to believe almost anything.

"Where did you meet Graham?" I asked him.

"At a sale." The bluster had gone out of him and if he hadn't been so unpleasant I might have felt some sympathy for him. "It was in a hotel and we had a few drinks beforehand."

"I suppose you told him you needed money and had some pictures you couldn't sell? When did he suggest faking the robbery?"

"That was later."

When Graham was sure of his man. He might have been prepared to take a chance but not Bridgeman; he liked everything a hundred percent safe. No loose ends.

"He told you when to go out and he'd fix everything else? You were to get twenty thousand pounds."

"How did you know?"

"That doesn't matter; I do know."

Twenty thousand plus the insurance. But very likely the pictures hadn't been insured. All the same, I still couldn't see why he hadn't sold them legitimately. Even if they couldn't be exported, he would still have got far more than that for them.

I asked him. At first I thought he wasn't going to answer. His eyes darted about as if he were looking for a way out. But there wasn't one and after a few seconds he capitulated.

"Who are you?" he demanded.

"I told you yesterday."

"You're nothing to do with the police?"

"No."

"The pictures weren't mine. My wife's father left them to her on condition that when she died they went to some bloody museum trust. Mean old bastard."

So that was it. His wife had died six months ago; the trust wouldn't have demanded the paintings immediately but he knew time was running out. He needed money badly and apart from the two pictures the only thing of any value he hadn't already sold was the snuffbox. I wondered what quirk of character had led him to keep that. Something to do with the trappings of a gentleman? If so it explained why he was so furious when he found Graham had taken that too. "Twisting bastards!" he had said. At the time it had seemed an odd turn of phrase.

"How did you find out about the gallery?" I asked him.

"Graham said something once when he'd had a few drinks. He told me there wouldn't be any problem about getting rid of the pictures."

It was as well for Graham that Bridgeman hadn't known. Not that it had made any difference in the end. And he knew now.

"Are you going home?"

He nodded.

We were somewhere near Marble Arch. I told the driver to put me down and take Williamson on to Paddington. He pulled into the kerb and I got out. Williamson could pay the fare.

The last I saw of him he was huddled in a corner of the seat, staring miserably into space. Perhaps he was looking into the future. If so, it can't have seemed very bright. The taxi pulled out into the stream of traffic heading west. I turned and started walking back to where I had left my car.

I knew for certain now that Fucillo was involved in

Bridgeman's racket. The girl, Kay, too. But who was the brains behind it, who ran the show? Until now I had assumed it was Bridgeman, but it was Fucillo who had dealt with Williamson and when he spoke to Kay about Bridgeman his tone hadn't suggested he was the boss. At the party I had wondered if Bridgeman was the strong man he liked people to believe; pomposity was usually a failing of the weak and small-minded and whoever had planned this operation wasn't either.

So was it Fucillo? On Saturday, when they were talking on the lawn, he could have been giving Bridgeman orders, not the other way round.

But what had Rekha been doing at the gallery? And why had she walked past me as if we had never met? I was puzzled and depressed.

TWELVE

That evening I had a visitor. I was using the washing machine in the old scullery and I didn't hear the bell; possibly she hadn't rung it. When I went back to the kitchen she was standing there looking round with apparent interest. Stephanie Bridgeman, in scarlet pants and a top that was almost transparent.

Her hair hung in blond waves to her shoulders and her lips matched her trousers glossily. Given a sultry glance she would have looked like something out of a forties film. But her expression was friendly.

"Hi," she said.

"Hallo." I shut the door to cut down the noise of the machine. I wasn't very pleased to see her. "I didn't hear the bell."

From the way she smiled I guessed I had been right and she hadn't bothered with formality. Very neighbourly. She should teach her father the art sometime. But his men didn't trouble with bells either.

"I thought it was time we got to know each other better," she explained, "so I came to say hallo."

I grinned. "Hallo, Miss Bridgeman."

"For God's sake! I'm Stephanie. Or Steph. Have I interrupted you?"

"No, I was only doing some washing. It can look after itself now. Wonderful thing, automation."

"Yes." She looked round again. "Where's your dog? You have one, haven't you?"

"Somebody shot him," I said.

She frowned, as if she suspected I was joking. Then she saw I wasn't. "Oh no! Was he ill or something?"

"No, he was fine. I came home last night and found him lying on the floor there with a bullet in his head. Just about where you're standing."

Involuntarily she looked down.

"That's horrible."

The trouble with actors, I thought, is that you can't tell when they're not acting. But I was pretty sure the shock in her eyes was genuine.

"Somebody broke in and he went for them," I told her. "He had a piece of their trousers in his teeth."

I was watching her but she didn't show any reaction. Either she didn't know about her father's men coming here or she was a better actress than I suspected.

"How about a drink?" I asked her.

"May I have a scotch?"

I was relieved she hadn't asked for anything more exotic; my cellar was restricted in range as well as quantity. Whisky and beer. We went into the living-room and I poured one of each.

"Water?" I asked. "Or something else?" I had some bottles of ginger ale.

"As it comes, please."

How old was she? I wondered. Nineteen? Not that that meant anything. I must be getting old myself to think it should. We sat down in the two easy chairs, half facing each other. She raised her glass.

"Cheers."

"Cheers," I said.

Her eyes, fringed by thick false lashes, watched me over

the rim. A smile hovered round the corners of her perfect mouth. She wasn't wearing a bra and I could see the gentle rise and fall of her small breasts.

"I phoned you earlier," she said.

"Oh?"

"To see if you'd be at home if I came. Then, when the rain stopped, I thought I might as well come anyway."

"I didn't hear your car."

"I walked."

She had stretched out her legs and I glanced at her feet. She couldn't have walked far in those flimsy sandals and it was nearly a mile round by the road.

"I did. Honestly." She smiled, daring me to contradict her, then she looked round the room. "Isn't it lonely here on your own?"

The directness of youth, I thought. She made me feel about fifty.

"Sometimes," I admitted. "Not often."

"Now?"

"How could it be with you here?" Keep it flippant, I told myself. But her presence wasn't helping. Apart from anything else, she was too attractive.

"How long is it since your wife died?" she asked.

"Three years."

"Do you still miss her?"

Only one person could ask me that: Rekha, who this afternoon had treated me as if I were a stranger. Stephanie hadn't the right. But she hadn't meant it to be an intrusion, she was just too young to understand. Too insensitive. She would never be a good actress.

"Yes, I miss her," I said. It came out more curtly than I had intended and to make amends I asked her if she would like another drink.

"Yes, please."

She stood up to give me her glass and tripped over her high heels. Or perhaps she caught her foot in the rug. Or neither and she did it on purpose. Whichever it was, she nearly fell and grabbed at me to save herself. My glass was still a quarter full and the beer spilled down the front of her blouse.

She looked up, still clinging to me. Her eyes were bright and she was laughing.

"I'm sorry, Clive," she said lightly.

"I'm not." It was a joke, silly, meaning nothing.

"Aren't you?" She moved her arms up to my neck and pressed herself a little harder against me. Her lips brushed my mouth.

She knew what she was doing. Perhaps she liked playing with fire, seeing how far she could go before drawing back at the last moment. A tease. Then I remembered Foskett going up the stairs and her telling him they hadn't long.

"Clive," she murmured, drawling it out.

"Yes?"

"Nothing. Just Clive."

Her mouth moved against mine disturbingly. To hell with common sense. Why not, if that was what she wanted?

Maybe I was revenging myself on Rekha. But something warned me the game would be too dangerous. For all I knew, Bridgeman had sent Stephanie here. Just as he had told her to pump me the other day.

"We'd better mop you up," I said lightly. "If we don't you'll smell like a brewery when it dries."

She sighed. "All right."

I started towards the kitchen to fetch a cloth but she stopped me.

"Here you are." She reached up and undid something. The flimsy top fell away and she held it out to me. She had firm, proud young breasts.

I took the blouse, found a clean cloth in the kitchen and sponged out the dark stain. I was still doing it when I heard her heels tapping on the tiles. I looked round. She was holding out the red trousers. Apart from a pair of very abbreviated briefs and her sandals she was naked.

"There's some on these as well," she said.

"Very convenient."

"Yes, isn't it?" She grinned. I handed her the blouse and took her trousers. "You're very domesticated, aren't you?"

"Force of circumstances," I said. A fivepence piece would have covered the stain. I wiped it out and handed the trousers back to her. "Why did you really come here tonight?"

"I was bored."

"Thanks. Is sex the only cure you know?"

She eyed me provocatively, making no move to put her trousers on. "Do you know a better one?"

"Not better, different. Is your father at home?"

"Yes. Why?"

"I thought perhaps he suggested you come."

I was willing to bet her surprise was genuine. Then she laughed. "Him send me? You must be out of your mind. He'd go up the wall if he knew I was here like this."

I tossed the cloth on to the draining-board and went back to the living-room. Stephanie followed.

"You're very close to him, aren't you?" I remarked.

"What makes you say that?"

"I've seen you together."

"We get on. We don't see much of each other."

"What about your mother? What would she say if she knew?"

"God knows. Anyway, she isn't my mother, she's a step. They were only married a couple of years ago. She understands me better than he does but I can't get round her like

I can him. She isn't there now, she's gone out somewhere, so she won't know."

"You get on with them?"

"They're okay. But they're so bloody old-fashioned."

The generation gap. A different way of looking at things. Was it only the pill responsible for that?

"We could have fun," she said.

I didn't doubt it. But that was hardly the point as things were.

"Not tonight," I told her. Nor any other time, I thought. "Sorry."

"Is there something wrong with you?" She didn't sound angry or contemptuous. More interested.

I grinned. "Not in the way you mean."

She grinned back. "I could tell that."

Perhaps she was right and there was something the matter with me. Was I living too much in the past, recognising a duty that no longer existed to someone who wasn't there to ask it? Who wouldn't be hurt whatever I did?

But I knew that if Stephanie had been Rekha Graham that wouldn't have counted.

"Let's forget it," I suggested.

Anger sparked in her big blue eyes. "I'm not used to being given the brush-off."

"Chalk it up as a new experience then." It was my turn to be bored and I wanted her to go.

"You offered me another drink." Her anger had faded as quickly as it came and she was smiling again.

"Maybe it wasn't such a good idea."

I went to the door and looked out. It was raining again, harder than ever.

"You'll get wet," I told her.

Our eyes met, hers mocking and triumphant. "You'll drive me home, Clive, won't you?"

"Why?"

"You mean you'd let me walk all that way? In these?" She raised one delicately shod foot.

"You walked here," I pointed out. "At least, you said you did."

She grinned. "Lew gave me a lift to the village. I told him I was going to see a friend and he and Andrews were going that way anyhow."

Andrews, I thought. Matey. It had to be.

"Anyway," Stephanie said, "it's raining. I'd get soaked."

"You could try hitching," I suggested. "Somebody might go past."

"Pig!"

I laughed. "All right, I'll take you."

She began pulling on her trousers. They were tight and she had to slip off her sandals but this time she didn't grab at me for support. I waited while she put on her blouse, then we went out to the yard. I had fixed the back door this morning; there didn't seem much point in locking it but I did all the same.

The barn was warm and dry and smelt of corn. I got into the Ford, switched on the lights and opened the other door for Stephanie. She climbed in gracefully.

We bumped down the track and onto the lane.

"How well did you know Graham?" I demanded.

I had hoped the sudden question might catch her off guard but she didn't seem disconcerted by it.

"How did you know I knew him?" she asked.

"That night when he crashed and you came running over you cried out, 'Ricky!' "

"Did I? We sort of lived together, off and on. A few months ago. It didn't last long."

So why had she expected him to drop in that evening?

Unless her father had told her he was coming or she had heard it from one of the others. Overheard it, probably.

"Did your father know about it?" I asked.

"Not likely! If he had he'd have been so mad he'd have—" She stopped abruptly.

"He'd have what?"

"Made me give up my flat." She meant he paid the rent. "He has this thing about morals."

Like hell he had, I thought. He probably made her a generous allowance too; she would hate to lose that.

I turned onto the main road, then almost immediately left up the drive to the house.

"You'd better come in," Stephanie said ungraciously when I stopped the Ford in front of it. She got out and started towards the front door without waiting to see if I followed.

I wasn't anxious to meet Bridgeman just then but I was curious. Beyond the garage a thin crack of light showed under the door of the rear shed.

We were halfway across the hall when a door on the right opened and Foskett came out. Seeing Stephanie he stopped, his face clouding angrily.

"Where've you been?" he demanded, ignoring me.

"Out." Her manner blended contempt and defiance. And something else. Pleasure?

"With him?" Foskett looked at me.

"What the hell has it to do with you?"

Until then I had assumed he objected because I knew what was going on and being with me was consorting with the enemy, now I realised it was more personal. He was jealous. So jealous that for the moment he hardly cared what he said or did.

"I'm not having you—" he began furiously.

"*You're* not having!" Stephanie's tone was pure contempt

now. "Who the hell do you think you are? Just because once I let you—"

She stopped in midsentence. The door behind Foskett had opened and Bridgeman was standing there.

"Get out!" he told his manager. He had spoken quietly but his tone made me feel cold.

For perhaps five seconds they stared at each other and I thought Foskett was going to bluster. Then he turned and strode out of the house. The front door slammed behind him with a thud.

"What have you been up to with him?" Bridgeman demanded. Either he hadn't noticed me yet or he was too angry to care.

"Nothing much," Stephanie muttered sulkily.

"What does that mean?"

"It wasn't anything."

At that moment I realised two things: first, that Stephanie was scared of her father and, second, that he still didn't know what she was. Perhaps he guessed, and the suspicion was torturing him now. For the first time he looked at me.

"If you've been—" he began.

It was like a scene from some Victorian melodrama and I wished I could laugh. Only it wasn't funny. Then Stephanie giggled, a high-pitched sound that grated on my nerves.

"You needn't worry," she told him, "Clive's a perfect little gentleman."

In the second's silence that followed I heard a key being pushed into the lock of the front door. We all looked that way. The door opened and Eunice Bridgeman walked in wearing a shirt and slacks and flat shoes. She stopped just inside the hall, taking in the little scene.

"Why, Clive, how nice to see you!" she said. She closed the door and came farther into the hall. It struck me there was something wary, watchful in her manner, and I wondered if she had become accustomed to acting as a buffer between her husband and Stephanie.

"He brought me home," the latter said. "That's all. I can't think what all the inquest's about."

I remembered what she had told me about her mother understanding more than her father. Now, strangely, it seemed to me Eunice was in charge of the situation. Perhaps that wasn't really so surprising; Bridgeman could handle plenty of situations but I doubted if he was equipped to deal with an oversexed daughter.

"Well, I'll say good night," Stephanie announced brightly. She started up the stairs, bouncing a little as if to show us what had happened hadn't bothered her. But I knew she was whistling in the dark. She had been scared.

"I'll go," I said. "Good night."

They didn't try to stop me.

Outside there was no sign of Foskett. No sign of anyone. The rain had stopped. I paused, listening, but the only sound was the drip of moisture from the trees. I walked quickly to the corner of the house; the light in the rear shed had been switched off.

There was another car parked beside my Cortina now, a dark blue Jaguar. The car that had followed me yesterday morning. The bodywork was splashed with mud almost up to the windows. I rubbed the tips of my fingers along it and looked at them; they were almost red. And the engine was still hot.

Puzzled, I got into the Cortina and drove home.

THIRTEEN

The questions haunted me. However hard I tried to concentrate on other things, always I came back to them. They were unavoidable. Why had Rekha gone to the gallery that afternoon? And why, when she saw me there, had she behaved as if I were a stranger?

She had told me she had never met Fucillo, yet he had greeted her like an old friend. It didn't make sense. Or rather, it made horrible sense. I just didn't want to face the truth.

It was less than a week since we first met—we were almost strangers. All I knew about her was what she had told me herself. There was only her word for it that she and Graham had parted, that they hadn't still been partners in more senses than one. Was that why she had gone to see Bridgeman after the crash?

Perhaps Graham hadn't been her husband and that was a lie too.

If so, she was involved in the art thefts. Almost certainly she had told Bridgeman everything I knew or suspected about his operation. It wasn't a pleasant thought. If I hadn't met her by chance like that at the gallery I would probably have rung her this evening to tell her what I had learnt from Williamson. That I hadn't was something to be thankful for. There wasn't much else.

She must have been laughing up her sleeve at me all the time. I had swallowed everything she told me. Even at first, when I hadn't liked her, it hadn't occurred to me she was lying.

The other night in the wood Foskett must have shot her by mistake when he was aiming at me. I remembered how she had switched on her torch, revealing me in the darkness. And yesterday she had gone with me to see Williamson, playing out the charade.

I poured myself a scotch and drank it neat, slumped in a chair and telling myself there must be some other explanation. There wasn't; it all fitted too well.

Or if there was, I couldn't see it.

All I could understand was Rekha walking past me like that with a cold "Excuse me," and the way she and Fucillo had greeted each other.

I should have accepted what Stephanie offered. She was an attractive, exciting girl. Perhaps she had been right and we could have had fun.

I finished my drink and went to bed. I slept badly and woke in the small hours haunted by the memory of Rekha on the way back from Somerset. Of the laughter in her eyes and her lips on mine.

Eventually I dozed off again and woke soon after seven. My head ached but apart from some tenderness my side was a lot better. I put on my glasses and walked over to the window. It was a fine, sunny morning, the air clear and the countryside clean and fresh after the rain. I wished I didn't feel so bloody depressed.

Brandy had always ambled across when I entered the kitchen and this morning I missed him. I crossed the yard and walked up the track to a field of winter barley. The day was already warm; soon it would be really hot. I picked an ear of the barley and rolled it between my hands, separating the corn from the chaff. There hadn't been enough rain to do any harm and the corn was firm and dry. Tomorrow, if the weather held, we should be able to start combining. Foskett had started yesterday; I had seen two machines at work in one of the fields by the road when I came back from London. It seemed odd that work on Langley Farm could go on as usual in spite of everything.

By the time I got back to the house the paper had come and I took it through to the kitchen to read while I had breakfast. A headline near the foot of the front page caught my eye: "ART RAID VICTIM FOUND SHOT."

The report was brief. Colonel Arthur Williamson had been found dead by his servant at his home, the Old Manor House, Culcombe, Somerset, late last night. No weapon had been found and the police were treating the case as murder.

I hadn't liked Williamson and he had become mixed up with Bridgeman and Fucillo through his own greed but he hadn't deserved to die for that. He must have been killed because he had gone to the gallery; once they discovered he knew its connection with the robberies he was as good as dead.

Then I saw something else: Rekha had seen me following him. She must have told Fucillo and he or one of Bridgeman's men had driven down to Somerset. That would account for the mud on the Jaguar; the soil round Culcombe was nearly red. I felt slightly sick.

I supposed I should go to the police. But what could I tell them? Suspicions weren't evidence and there was little enough in the way of hard facts. If Rekha's flat and my house had been ransacked, they would ask, why hadn't we reported it at the time? Miserably I remembered that it was Rekha who had said there wasn't much point. The search had been a red herring to divert suspicion from her. She must have rung Bridgeman from the service area at Membury or the pub where we had lunch to tell him the flat would be empty. It had been her suggestion that we not drive straight back. Only we had still arrived too early.

At least she hadn't bargained for my being beaten up, I thought. Her shock had been genuine. It wasn't much but I was glad of that.

Now she would probably deny everything that had happened. And the police would believe her. She had a responsible, highly paid job and, no doubt, useful friends. It would throw doubt on everything else I told them. They would dismiss the search here and Brandy's killing as the work of vandals out for an evening's kicks. Tearaways didn't normally carry guns but I wasn't going to dig him up to show them the wound.

Nor were they likely to be impressed merely because Graham had hired a plane on the days the robberies had been committed; he had flown on plenty of other occasions when nothing had happened. The police didn't like trouble-makers. Especially trouble-makers who tried to teach them their job.

I knew I was finding excuses for not going to them. Avoiding the issue because the real reason I didn't want to go was Rekha. It didn't matter that she had deceived me, she was involved and I didn't want to be responsible for her being arrested. Probably going to gaol. Not after Sunday.

But what had happened then to make any difference? We had talked and she had kissed me. Stop. Not exactly passionate embraces either. I had no one to blame but myself if I had thought they meant anything.

One thing was more than ever certain now: I had to know the truth. Not just part of it, everything. However much I might hate what I learnt. I couldn't simply shut my eyes and hope it would go away, it wouldn't. Williamson was dead because he had known too much. Maybe I would be next.

I finished my breakfast and went out to talk to Fred and

Tom. Fred might be a stockman but he had worked on
farms twice as long as I had and I wanted his opinion about
starting the harvest tomorrow. If he agreed, Tom could
start getting everything ready. For the next two or three
weeks I would be too busy to worry about Bridgeman and
Fucillo.

We walked up to the field together, Fred setting the pace
with his deliberate, plodding strides. In spite of the heat he
was wearing a jacket and his old cap pulled down low over
his forehead. I knew Tom was looking forward to the harvest even more than I was. For me it was the return for
months of planning and work, the outlay on fertilisers, seed
and wages. Basically commercial, even if you couldn't alto-
gether eliminate the sentiment. For him it was the climax of
the year. He would be in control up there on the seat of the
lumbering combine. It was dry, dusty work but he would
revel in it and laugh that it gave him a good thirst. We
weren't a bad team.

"It's about ready," Fred declared, examining the corn in
the palm of his hand, then stooping stiffly to study the
growing barley. It had a warm, sweet scent.

"Tomorrow then, if it keeps fine?" I suggested. It was my
responsibility but we were all involved.

Fred nodded. Tom followed suit sagely.

"Right," I said. Now the decision had been taken I felt a
mild elation.

We walked back down the track together. I was conscious
of a new restlessness, a sense of urgency I hadn't felt before, as if subconsciously I knew matters were moving to a
climax. Williamson's death had been an indication.

And Fucillo had said he was only here for a few days.

Fucillo. He had told the girl at the gallery Bridgeman
must get some picture, it was worth a lot to them. What
picture?

When we reached the yard I left the others and went into the house to phone Bill Mackay's office. I had an idea and I wanted to put it to the test as soon as possible. They said he was standing in for the night man and I'd probably find him at home.

I did.

"Do you know if there's been another of those art robberies in the last few days?" I asked him.

"There hasn't."

"You sound very sure."

I could almost hear him grin. "I am. I've looked out for anything since you rang."

"Could you let me know if there is? Right away?"

"What is all this, Clive?" I should have remembered journalists had an overdeveloped sense of curiosity. "What's going on?"

"I'll tell you sometime," I promised. "Will you do it?"

"Okay," he agreed.

"As soon as you hear?"

"If it's so important, I just hope it's in the middle of the night." He paused. "People don't really play amateur detectives, you know. You sound as if you've been reading too many thrillers."

"Could be," I agreed. "Thanks, Bill."

I wasn't playing amateur detectives, I was protecting myself. And checking up on Rekha. Put like that it didn't seem a very praiseworthy occupation.

Oh hell! I thought.

She rang while I was having lunch. Bread and cheese and a can of beer. I swallowed a mouthful and went to answer the phone.

"Clive?"

"Yes?"

"Are you feeling better?"

"I'm fine."

"Oh." There was a distinct pause. "I thought you sounded different."

How did she expect me to sound? Perhaps she thought I was too stupid to put two and two together and get the right answer.

"Why did you ring?" I asked her.

She ignored that. Attack is the best method of defence. "I suppose it's yesterday afternoon." Her tone was hardly apologetic. More accusing.

"That and other things," I agreed.

"What do you mean, other things?"

"It doesn't matter." Who did I think I was fooling? But I had no intention of explaining.

"Very well." It was exactly right, blending regret and impatience perfectly. "I rang to tell you Bridgeman came to a sale this morning. He bought a picture. I thought you might be interested."

Why should I be? He must often buy pictures for his gallery or legitimate customers. Why ring just to tell me now? Unless she had hoped to find out how much I had guessed.

"What was it?" I asked.

"A portrait of a woman by a French artist named Leclerc. He died about 1900. Bridgeman paid nearly nine thousand pounds for it. According to him he bought it for an American collector. That means he'll have to get an export licence."

"Will he get it?"

"Oh yes. It's not a very interesting picture."

I still couldn't see why she was telling me.

"I can't see it means anything," I remarked. If I didn't show any interest it would sound suspicious. "Can you?"

"I don't know. He was so keen to get it. There was a woman there; I'd never seen her before and nobody seemed to know her. She wanted it and forced the price up. There were only the two of them bidding and I expected him to drop out long before it went so high."

"Harry's got to get that picture," Fucillo had said. Was this the one? And why?

"You think it has something to do with the others?" I asked.

"Don't you?"

"I don't know," I admitted. I wished I could rid myself of the feeling I was behaving badly.

"What did you do last night?" Rekha enquired. I could tell she wanted me to think she didn't care. It was almost laughable because I knew she didn't.

"Stephanie came round." She could make what she liked of that.

"You must have had a cosy evening. Are you . . . ?"

"Am I what?"

"Nothing. It doesn't matter either. Goodbye."

"Goodbye," I said.

I replaced the phone and the next moment wished I hadn't; she had offered no explanation for her behaviour yesterday afternoon. Perhaps she didn't care what I thought. And like a fool I had let her see I didn't trust her any more.

I stood there thinking about what she had told me. It was on the cards Bridgeman had wanted me to know about his buying the picture and told her to ring me but I didn't see why he should. If this was the painting Fucillo had told Kay he must get, why was it worth so much to them? On the face of it, it seemed unlikely.

But if it wasn't, there must be another. I wondered how long it would be before I heard from Bill Mackay.

FOURTEEN

The restless feeling persisted all that day. I was irritable, out of sorts with myself and the world at large. And knowing why didn't help. The only consolation was that the weather held; we should be able to start the harvest tomorrow.

It was just before eight o'clock and I had finished my supper when I heard a knock on the back door and a man's voice called. "You about, Clive?"

Peter. I wondered what he wanted; he didn't often come to see me these days.

"Come in," I shouted.

He looked as if his weekend thrash hadn't been ended for very long. Until about a year ago he had done his best to keep up appearances so that, except when he was actually drunk, his drinking showed only in his eyes. Lately he had stopped bothering. This evening it would have been hard to say exactly what it was about him that looked the worse for wear but the overall effect was a mess. It was as though the edges were blurred. I took him into the living-room and pushed one of the chairs forward. If he was hoping for a drink he would be unlucky.

"What's brought you here?" I asked. I didn't mean to sound unwelcoming but I probably succeeded. I wasn't in the mood for company, especially his.

"I wanted to talk to you."

Oh no! My spirits sank even lower. A man-to-man talk with Peter was something I could do without.

"What about?" I asked him, wondering how long it would be before he forgot his reason for coming and departed in a haze of alcohol. That had happened before. But he sounded more sober than he looked.

Fond though I was of Peter, I found it hard to sympathise with his moods at the best of times. It was easier to be angry with him for wasting himself; he used to be a good farmer. And for hurting Elizabeth. She might be a raving snob but she had her good qualities and she loved him. Besides, this wasn't one of the best of times. I wished he would come to the point and go.

"Harry Bridgeman," he said distinctly.

Whatever I had expected it wasn't that. "What about him?" I demanded. I hoped to God Peter hadn't stumbled on something; that would make everything more complicated than it was already.

He shifted in his chair and looked hopefully at the sideboard. "Can I have a drink?"

"No," I said.

He didn't complain; he must have known I would refuse. "Harry says you're being a nuisance."

My brother was certainly full of surprises this evening. "How?" I demanded.

Peter looked more embarrassed than ever. "You'll say it's no business of mine. He doesn't like your hanging round Stephanie. He says she doesn't either but you won't leave her alone."

I felt like bursting out laughing. "You'd better tell him to suggest she leave me alone," I said. "It's about time he learnt what she is."

Anyway, what the hell was Peter doing, running errands like this for Bridgeman?

"I know," he muttered.

"I've spoken to her twice," I told him. "Once at that bloody awful party I took Elizabeth to because you weren't in a fit state to take her yourself and the other time when she came here last night and wanted to climb into bed with me. I drove her home."

"Is that all?"

"Yes. And he knows it is."

"I thought maybe you'd . . ." He stopped. "I couldn't see her minding. Anyway, I've told you what he said."

"Why? If he wanted to tell me a load of crap like that, why didn't he come himself? Or ring me up?"

"He thought, as we were brothers—"

I said something brief and obscene. "Why send you, Peter? He must have had some reason."

My brother almost squirmed in his chair. His eyes went to the sideboard again. "Can I tell him you won't have anything more to do with her?" he pleaded. "You know how he dotes on her."

Even the Mafiosi were fond fathers, I'd heard.

My heart seemed to miss a beat. Was that it? Were the Mafia behind Bridgeman's racket? If so, Fucillo was one of them and I was stirring up even more trouble than I'd realised.

"You still haven't explained why you're acting as his messenger boy," I said, pushing the thought away.

"I owe him some money," Peter muttered.

So that was it. Bridgeman had sent a message in code. He hadn't meant Stephanie; he knew I wasn't playing around with her. He was warning me not to interfere in his affairs.

"How much?" I asked.

"Twelve thousand."

"You bloody fool!"

"I had to have it. Everything went wrong last year and the

bank wouldn't let me have any more; they hinted I'd better sell the farm. I was telling Harry about it and he offered to lend it to me. I said no at first but he was so keen to help . . ."

I could imagine. Probably at the time Bridgeman had had no more in mind than bribing Peter to ease his way into local society. But even then he must have seen the loan as a lever he might find useful one day.

"Did he say what he'd do if I didn't take any notice?" I asked.

"No. But I don't want to upset him, Clive; he might turn nasty."

"You're damn right he might," I agreed.

It was blackmail. If I didn't leave him alone he would put the screws on Peter. That would mean his selling the farm and within a year or two he'd drink himself to death.

There was only one bright spot in the whole depressing picture: Bridgeman must be worried.

"Tell him I don't know what he's talking about and he can go to hell," I said roughly.

"For God's sake, Clive. Look at it—"

"I don't have to look. It's a bluff. And it's nothing to do with Stephanie."

"What do you mean?"

"Nothing you need worry about," I told him. "How did you come?"

He still looked worried and uncertain. "In the car."

"I'll drive you home."

"I can manage."

"It's not you I'm thinking about, it's the people you might meet on the way," I said unkindly.

We went out through the kitchen.

"Where's Brandy?" Peter asked, looking round vaguely.

"One of Bridgeman's men shot him."

He stared at me.

"You have some nice friends," I said.

I could have shown him the bruises on my body, still a picturesque black, blue and yellow, but what was the point?

His car was in the yard. I held out my hand for the keys and after groping in his pockets for a few seconds he found them and handed them over.

Elizabeth greeted us without any marked enthusiasm and I wondered if Peter had told her what Bridgeman had said about my annoying Stephanie.

"Look," I told her, irritated by her disapproval, "do you think I'd play around with that little—" I stopped myself in time, Elizabeth didn't like the sort of language I had been going to use. And what was I being so priggish about? It wasn't moral scruples that had stopped me accepting Stephanie's invitation.

"Why did you have to choose her?" Elizabeth retorted angrily. Clearly she either hadn't heard what I said or didn't believe me.

I understood then. It wasn't my sex life that concerned her, it was what she saw as the danger to Peter that might result from it. And to her.

"I didn't choose her," I told her roughly. "I've hardly spoken to her. Be your age, Elizabeth."

It was a tactless thing to say, my sister-in-law had just had her fortieth birthday and she was touchy about her age. She flushed.

"I'm going home," I said.

She didn't offer to drive me so I walked. I had gone fifty yards or so down the lane when I met an Allegro Estate coming the other way, Eunice Bridgeman's car. She saw me and waved. When I glanced back she was turning in at Peter's gate.

Walking gave me plenty of time to think about the impli-

cations of what he had said. He might irritate me, anger me
sometimes, but still I was fond of him and I didn't want him
to suffer because of anything I did. Should I give up annoying Bridgeman? After all, what business was it of mine?

But I didn't like being blackmailed. Bridgeman was bluff-
ing, I was the target, not Peter, and if he carried out his
implied threat he would lose his hold over me.

Then something occurred to me and I stopped, appalled.
Peter had admitted he was in Bridgeman's hands inasmuch
as he had borrowed twelve thousand pounds he couldn't
hope to repay for a long time if ever, but had he told me the
whole truth? Was he mixed up in the stolen picture racket
too? He had told Elizabeth that Bridgeman was "all right"
and she had implied they saw a fair amount of each other.
Perhaps Bridgeman had blackmailed him too, forcing his
silence, if nothing more active.

A few days ago the suspicion wouldn't have occurred to
me. I would have been angered by any suggestion that
Peter was capable of anything dishonest, let alone criminal.
He was a fool to himself, maybe, but as straight as anyone I
knew. Now I could no longer be so confident. I wasn't sure
of anything.

I told myself that if he was involved and I persisted in
hounding Bridgeman and the others I might end up being
responsible for convicting my own brother. Was I prepared
to risk that? But he was in danger anyway, very likely more
danger.

Unless . . .

I still didn't know who ran the whole operation. Was it
possible the brain behind it all was Peter's? He was no fool
intellectually; at school and university he had done a good
deal better than I had. If so, his bouts of drunkenness were
faked and it was hard to believe that. As hard, almost, as to

believe Peter capable of being mixed up in theft and murder.

Bridgeman, Fucillo, now Peter. And Rekha? Why the hell had I ever started meddling in this bloody business? But I knew I couldn't stop now. It was too late.

There was a car parked in front of my house. She was standing looking across to the wood as she had done the first time she came. I was surprised how much the sight of her hurt and had to suppress a childish temptation to walk past without speaking. I stopped and she walked over.

"Hallo, Clive."

Her eyes were dark, solemn, and I couldn't read the expression in them.

"I wasn't expecting you," I said. It sounded ruder than I had meant it to.

"No, I don't suppose you were." She sighed almost inaudibly.

Whatever else she might be, I told myself bitterly, she was a first-rate actress.

I unlocked the back door and stood aside for her to go in. The remains of my supper were still on the table but this evening I didn't care what the place looked like.

She was waiting for me to ask her to sit down and I moved a chair for her ungraciously. Behaving badly was a sop to my feelings.

"Perhaps I shouldn't have come," she observed. Her back was to the light and I couldn't see the expression in her eyes. "It would have been embarrassing if you'd had Stephanie Bridgeman here."

"Why did you come?" I demanded. I didn't have to explain to her about Stephanie; she could think what she liked.

"Because I wanted to see you. You sounded so strange on the phone, angry and bitter."

"That's hardly surprising, is it?"

"Because of what happened at the gallery, you mean? But you said there were other things."

"What were you doing there?"

For a second or two she faced me defiantly and I thought she was going to demand what right I had to ask. She must have decided it would be bad tactics, for she said simply, "I wanted to see what it was like. What pictures he had. I'd never been there before."

"Why?"

"Because I was curious. And I thought it might be useful to know." She paused. "Why were you there, Clive?"

"The same reason." I was remembering how assured she had seemed and how quickly she had recovered from the shock of seeing me. "You told Fucillo I'd followed Williamson, didn't you?"

"No, of course not. Why should I? Anyway, I didn't see Williamson."

"Somebody did and you were the only one who saw me. Didn't you know they murdered him last night?"

"Oh no!"

I could have sworn her surprise was genuine. Maybe they hadn't told her about that. But I was in no mood to be diverted by it. Then, as she realised what I was saying, the surprise gave way to anger.

"You think I—"

"Didn't you?"

"No."

"If you didn't . . ." I began.

Then I stopped. I had remembered something, something I should have thought of long before this. As I grabbed his arm to push him towards the taxi I had told Williamson Fucillo was behind us. He had looked over his shoulder and muttered, "Not Fucillo." At the time I hadn't taken any notice because I knew the American wasn't there. But he had seen something and whatever it was had scared him so badly he had almost fallen into the cab.

It couldn't have been Rekha—he had no reason to be frightened of her. Unlikely to have been the girl Kay. That left Bridgeman, on his way back to the gallery. And Rekha couldn't have told him I was following Williamson.

But there were still things I didn't understand.

"Why didn't you say anything when you saw me?" I asked.

"Because I saw a man I knew must be Fucillo behind you. He knew you and I didn't want them to connect us."

"You expect me to believe that?"

"That's up to you," Rekha said coldly.

"If Bridgeman had been there he would have recognised you."

"I knew he wasn't."

"How?"

"I telephoned him and said I would be at the tube station in five minutes. There was something I wanted to tell him about Derek but I didn't want to go to the gallery. It would take him at least ten minutes to walk to the station and back and he was bound to wait there a little while until he realised I wasn't going to turn up."

I laughed. It was as if something had been screwing me up inside and now the tension had gone. But Rekha wasn't laughing.

"Is that all the faith you have in me?" she asked.

"I'm sorry. I didn't want to believe it but . . ."

"I don't think being sorry is enough." She stood up. "I'd better go."

"No," I said. I was horribly afraid that if she went now I might not see her again.

"I'd rather. I don't think I'm in the mood for this sort of thing."

At that moment the phone rang.

"Blast!" I muttered.

"You'd better answer it," Rekha said.

I walked across and picked up the hand-set. It was Bill Mackay. He sounded very pleased with himself.

"You asked me to let you know if there was another of those art robberies," he began.

"Yes," I agreed, cursing him for ringing just now. Another ten minutes and it wouldn't have mattered.

"I promised I would."

"Yes."

I heard a movement behind me and looked over my shoulder. Rekha was going out to the kitchen.

"There's a man named Canadoc Glenn; he lives in Suffolk. He and his wife had been away at some congress in Paris. They weren't expected back until tomorrow but they got a message their son was ill and came home this evening. The servants were out and they found a picture missing. A Hogarth."

I almost whistled aloud. Was this the painting Fucillo had said Bridgeman must get? Certainly a Hogarth would be worth a great deal of money. Far more than nine thousand pounds. But why say Bridgeman must get it? Why not "we must"?

"Are you still there?" Bill asked.

"Yes."

He told me some more about the stolen painting but nothing that I could see helped. I thanked him and replaced the phone. I wanted to tell Rekha.

But when I went out to the kitchen she wasn't there. I ran out to the yard. The Jaguar had gone.

FIFTEEN

I felt as if fate had kicked me in the stomach hard. It wasn't a pleasant sensation and it didn't help that I knew it was my own fault. I had made a mess of everything. If Rekha wanted no more to do with me I had no-one to blame but myself.

I tried not to think about her and to concentrate on the pictures. She was convinced the portrait Bridgeman had bought had something to do with the robberies but I couldn't see what. According to him, he had wanted it for an American buyer. Wanted it so badly he had allowed a woman with more money than artistic knowledge to force up the price far beyond its real value. I kept remembering what Fucillo had said, "Harry's got to get that picture, Kay." Which picture had he meant, the portrait or the Hogarth?

Or both? But he had said "picture."

The more I thought about it the more convinced I became that Rekha was right and there was a link between them and the portrait was only important because of it. I wished I had asked her more about the Leclerc; I had been so obsessed with my suspicions I had hardly listened to what she wanted to tell me.

I worried at it until I could hardly think straight, then I went to bed.

I didn't expect to sleep—my brain was too active—but I was on the point of dropping off when I came to with a start. Climbing out of bed, I grabbed my dressing-gown from its hook on the door and went downstairs. Bill Mackay's number was in a notebook beside the telephone, I looked it up and dialled.

A man whose voice I didn't recognise answered and told me to "Hang on a minute." I waited impatiently. Then Bill said, "Hallo?"

"Clive, Bill," I told him. "Do you know how big the Hogarth painting that was stolen is?"

"Huh?"

"How big is it? Do you know?"

"I haven't the slightest bloody idea." His exasperation crackled on the line. "Look, Clive, we're busy just now."

"I'm sorry," I told him, "but it's important. Can you find out?"

"The size?"

"Yes." He wasn't a fool; the fact that he sounded like one showed his mind was on other things.

"I suppose so."

"Will you?"

"Look, Clive, what difference does it make?"

"All the difference," I told him. "If I'm right."

"All right." He sighed. "I'll ring you back if I have any joy."

"Thanks, Bill," I said.

I pressed the rest down and dialled Rekha's number, wondering if she was in bed and if she would put the receiver down when she heard my voice.

She didn't. And she answered so quickly she couldn't have been in bed.

"It's Clive," I told her.

There was a tiny pause before she said, "Oh."

It didn't get us far but at least she hadn't rung off.

"Why did you leave like that?"

"There didn't seem much point in my staying."

"I hoped you would."

"It's late, Clive. I was just going to bed. It won't help talking about it now."

"Don't go." I was afraid she would put the phone down before I had time to ask her. "Can you tell me how big the painting Bridgeman bought today was?"

Silence. After a moment she asked, "Are you serious?"

"Very."

"Then I can't."

"Not even roughly?"

"About three feet by two, I suppose."

"Thank you," I said.

"Why do you want to know?"

"I'll explain when I see you," I told her. Then I realised that sounded like blackmail. Whatever I said seemed to make things worse. "Sorry. If I'm right I'll let you know."

"Yes, that would be better," she agreed. But she didn't sound angry. "Good night, Clive."

"Good night," I said.

I was wearing only the thin dressing-gown and it was cool in the living-room. It might be a long time before Bill rang back. I went upstairs, changed into a shirt and trousers. Came down again and poured myself a can of beer. Picked up the morning's paper and started to do the crossword. Thirteen down was "In Suffolk a tasty root well placed in the theatre." Place names shouldn't be too difficult. To pass the time I went to the cupboard, fetched a map of Suffolk and spread it out on the table. Even then it took me several minutes to find Stradishall.

I was pencilling it in when the phone rang.

"Clive? The Hogarth was thirty-five inches by twenty-three," Bill said.

"Thanks." I breathed a sigh of relief. It looked as if I might be right.

"I hope it helps," he commented ironically.

"It does," I assured him. "I'm very grateful. Next time I see you I'll buy you a pint."

"Make it a large scotch."

"All right," I agreed. "Night."

So that was how they worked it. It must be; nothing else fitted.

Bridgeman wouldn't risk keeping the Hogarth at his place longer than necessary. Maybe it had already been moved. I thought that unlikely but if I was going to do anything it had to be tonight; tomorrow might be too late. The clock said nearly one o'clock; I decided to wait another half hour and sat down to think about it.

It wasn't a very profitable exercise. For one thing, if I were wrong I would have burnt my boats and there was no way I could cover my tracks. I would be committed up to the neck. Might even go to gaol. For another, it was dangerous. Bridgeman and Fucillo had already killed once; they weren't likely to baulk at a second murder.

The minutes dragged by. At twenty-five past I went upstairs and changed my slippers for tennis shoes. Coming down again I fetched a small cold chisel from the scullery and slipped it into my pocket with a torch. Satisfied I had everything I needed, I switched off the lights and let myself out of the house.

It was clear and far lighter than I liked. I considered going on foot in case Bridgeman had posted a guard and he heard my car but I didn't fancy carrying a picture three feet by two all the way home. Also, it would take too long.

I backed the Ford out of the barn and drove down the track to the lane. There was no other traffic and I drove on my sidelights. When I came to the lay-by I turned into it and stopped, switching off the ignition, then the lights. Making sure the chisel and torch were still in my pocket, I got out. I left the driver's door unlocked. It was hardly likely anyone would come this way and steal the car while I was gone and I had an uncomfortable suspicion that I might be in a hurry when I returned. It was very quiet, the only sound the hum of an occasional car on the main road.

There was no stile and it took me a minute or so to locate the gap in the hedge Rekha had discovered. When I found it I pushed a way through and set out for the house five or six hundred yards away.

Ahead and to my left I could make out the dark shape of the wood. I kept well to the east of it, below the line of the ridge, so that the fall of the ground would conceal me from anyone there. Bridgeman could hardly post a watch all the time but, if I was right, he had more to protect tonight. All the same, I reckoned any guard was more likely to be near the house.

After a minute or two I came to the drive and crossed it. Fortunately Bridgeman hadn't ploughed this part of the farm and the turf was dry and firm under my feet. Nor was there any livestock. I could have got past a few cows all right but sheep would have been a different matter.

The house loomed up ahead, seeming much bigger in the half-light. I was keyed up, my nerves tense. If there was a guard, he was almost certainly armed. Thank God Bridgeman didn't like dogs. I veered a little to the right, keeping close to the hedge that bordered the garden on that side. The house was in darkness but I could make out the silhouettes of the garage and the two sheds. Then they merged into the shadow of the house.

There was soil under my feet now but footprints were the last of my worries. I pushed between some shrubs and saw the corner Eunice had said was her favourite part of the garden just ahead. It was almost suspiciously quiet.

When I reached the back of the second shed I stopped. To my right, a dozen yards away, was the wall of the house. A first floor window was open and I wondered if anyone slept there. Hoped it wasn't Fucillo. Forcing the door was bound to make a noise and I guessed he slept as lightly as a cat.

My heart thudding, I crept along the side of the shed. Here in the shadow of the house it was too dark to see the door. I ran my hands over the smooth new wood, feeling for the edge. The door fitted closely but there was a tiny gap between it and the frame and the wood was soft pine. I took the chisel out of my pocket, shoved it hard into the space and levered.

Nothing happened. I swore silently and tried again, pulling as hard as I dared. I knew that if I used too much strength the door might give way with a crash. This time the wood began to splinter. Sweat stood out on my forehead, part exertion, mostly nerves. Then the screws holding the lock tore free. To me the noise seemed loud enough to wake everybody in the house and I stood still, waiting for a shout or footsteps running towards me. Ready to run myself.

But still nothing disturbed the silence. Hardly able to believe it, I stepped into the shed and closed the door behind me as best I could.

I had to risk using my torch now, shielding the light with my hand. A bench ran along the left-hand wall with a rack of tools and a light over it. The top was littered with picture frames and stretchers. I hardly noticed them; leaning against the end wall was a picture in an ornate frame. It was a portrait of a young woman, her shoulders bare and her hair drawn back severely from her forehead. Below her slender waist her gown billowed out over a crinoline. It was the picture Bridgeman had bought the morning before; it fitted Rekha's description too well to be anything else.

I had deliberately brought only a small torch; it didn't give much light and I stooped down to examine the portrait more closely. It had to be Leclerc's painting—it would be too much of a coincidence if Bridgeman had two almost identical pictures here. The colours, flesh tones and the rich dark red of the woman's gown, were softened and dimmed by a thin film of dirt.

Yet something about the picture wasn't right.

I licked my right forefinger and rubbed one corner of the canvas. The dirt came away on my skin. I had never seen the original but I was prepared to bet this was a copy.

Oh God! I thought. Bridgeman had fooled me.

For a moment I squatted there, too shaken to move. By this time the real painting was probably a hundred miles away.

But in that case, why had he gone to the lengths of leaving the copy for me to find?

It took me a few seconds to see the truth. Maybe my brain wasn't functioning too well. When I did I started to search the shed, looking for what I believed must be there. At any moment Bridgeman or one of his men might come and find me. Perhaps that was his intention and the copy was a trap. But it was too late to worry about that now. I couldn't leave without knowing.

The bench top fitted flush to the wall. The wall itself was rough brick but below the top it was smooth, lined with hardboard. I could think of only one reason why anybody should bother to line a wall like that where it was out of sight and leave the part that wasn't. I found the edge of one piece of hardboard, inserted a chisel I found in the rack of tools and levered carefully. The board came away with a soft ripping sound.

Behind it there was another picture. I pulled it out and stood it against the first one. They were almost identical. Almost but not quite.

Picking them up together wasn't easy. I switched off my torch, slipped it into my pocket and got out of there as quickly as I could, waiting only to wedge the door shut with a stone. It wouldn't deceive anybody who went right up to it but it might fool a casual glance.

There was still no sound from the house. I doubled back round the shed the way I had come and dived into the shelter of the bushes. The pictures were heavy and awkward to carry, too big to tuck under my arm so I had to hold them in front of me. That way you feel the weight more. By the time I was halfway to the hedge my arms were crying out for relief but I didn't dare stop.

The worst part was over but still I half expected to hear the sounds of pursuit behind me. The gap in the hedge was just ahead; I lifted the pictures high enough to clear the bushes and pushed my way through.

The Cortina was still where I had parked it. Laying the pictures in the back, I covered them with an old rug and slipped into the driving seat. Relief made me almost light-headed and I realised how tense I had been. Even so, I didn't switch on the headlights until I reached the main road.

I had covered about five miles on the motorway when I saw the Silver Shadow coming up behind me. The motorway was well lit all the way into London and there was no mistaking the reflection with the distinctive Rolls radiator grille. The big car was overhauling me fast and my heart sank. Was this how it was going to end? In anticlimax or worse? I should have taken a roundabout route; once he knew the paintings were gone, Bridgeman was bound to guess who had taken them and where I would go.

I pressed my foot hard on the accelerator and the Ford responded gallantly. But it was no more than a gesture; the Rolls had thirty miles an hour in hand. I waited for it to come up with me.

It drew level and I looked to see who was in it. The driver was alone, a burly middle-aged man with a bald head and glasses. No-one I knew. He glanced across briefly, then away again. The Rolls went past, staying in the fast lane.

I felt the tension ease out of me and told myself I couldn't go on like this alternating fear and relief. I slowed down to sixty, relaxed.

Nevertheless, at the next junction I left the motorway and took to the minor roads.

There was room to park outside Corhampton Court but I drove past and round two corners until I found a side entrance that was overhung by trees and backed the Cortina into it. Nobody was likely to want to use the entrance at this time of night and a passer-by would have to look pretty closely to see the car there.

All the same, I didn't risk leaving the pictures.

Rekha answered my third ring. The door opened on its chain and she looked round it, her eyes heavy with sleep. Then she saw who I was and they widened.

"Clive! What do you want?"

"I'm sorry it's so late," I told her, "but can I come in? It's important."

She misunderstood and frowned. Then she saw the pictures. "What have you got there?"

I turned one of them so that she could see it.

"Clive, no!" she said. But she took the chain off the door

and opened it wide enough for me to go in. "Where did you get it?"

"Bridgeman's shed."

"You must be mad."

"Probably," I agreed. I was beginning to think so myself. I waited while she replaced the chain, then followed her into the living-room.

"It's the picture he bought this morning, isn't it?"

"Yes. But why have you stolen it?"

I told her. She listened without interrupting.

"What are you going to do now?" she asked when I had finished.

"Take them both to the police. Will you come with me? They'll take more notice of you and they may ask questions I can't answer."

I expected her to hesitate. Perhaps refuse point-blank. Instead she said, "All right. Sit down and I'll put some clothes on."

I propped the pictures against the settee and sat. At the door she stopped and looked at me.

"You'll need all the moral support you can get if you're wrong."

More than moral support, I thought, although that would help; I'd need a damned good lawyer and a lot of luck.

She was back in five minutes wearing a summery cream trouser suit, her hair coiled up. I picked up the pictures.

The road outside was still deserted. Rekha looked round for my car.

"I left it round the corner," I explained.

Why did picture frames have to be so heavy? I was glad when we reached the Cortina and I could put them down. We climbed in and I started the engine. With any luck this was the last lap.

At the end of the road I turned left.

"The police station's the other way," Rekha said.

"We're going to Scotland Yard," I told her. I reckoned it would save time in the long run and, hopefully, result in action without my having to answer too many questions. Which just shows how wrong you can be.

We drove out of the quiet suburban roads into the busier streets that lead down to the West End. Here the traffic never stops, there is just less of it at night. The darkened buildings in Piccadilly Circus were garish with neon signs. Beyond were quieter, more dignified streets. I parked the car and we got out. The new Scotland Yard might be more efficient, I thought, eyeing its concrete and glass, but it lacked the character of the old building in Whitehall. It was like going to any big office.

We were escorted to a small room and asked to wait. After the tension and activity of the last two hours waiting was an anticlimax and I fretted impatiently. Rekha sat calmly, her eyes on the pictures propped against one leg of the table.

After a few minutes a man about my own age came in and introduced himself as Detective Sergeant Perring. He had a Londoner's accent and a reasonably friendly manner.

I explained as briefly as I could why we were there. He listened politely and when I finished nodded and said he would have a word with his chief inspector.

We waited again, longer this time.

"You're sure you're right, Clive?" Rekha asked. She looked unhappy and the fact that she had put it into words told me she was worried too.

"No," I admitted. "But I can't see any other way they could have worked it."

Perring returned accompanied by an older man. Detective Chief Inspector Rumbelow looked every inch a policeman; he was tall and square with a chest like a tank and daunting eyes under brows that jutted aggressively. A man who clearly saw no point in appearing friendly when he wasn't. He wasn't now. But he listened attentively enough while I repeated what I had told Perring.

Then he took me through it again. If he was interested he didn't show any sign of it. Except that this time he asked a good many questions.

"All right, Mr. Fordham," he said heavily when I had finished, "we'd better have a look." He turned to Perring. "Get Freddy Hutchinson, Frank."

The sergeant went out. Rumbelow was eyeing the pictures as if he resented their presence.

"You realise your position if you're wrong?" he asked flatly, turning to look at me.

I nodded. I was only too well aware of it.

Rekha stared at her hands. I noticed they were clutching her bag tightly and somehow that gave me a little comfort. At least she was concerned.

We waited again.

After five minutes or so Perring came back with a thin, elderly man carrying a small bag of tools.

"Okay, Freddy?" Rumbelow asked him.

"Yes, sir."

The old boy spread a cloth over the table and picked up the first picture. It was the copy. He eyed it curiously for a second or two and I wondered how much Perring had told him. Then he laid it down on the cloth and started removing the stretchers. After a few minutes they came away from the frame and he lifted out the canvas.

"Nothing 'ere," he reported. "It's not bad though, for what it is."

Nobody else said anything. He stood the painting on the floor and picked up the second one, studying it appreciatively.

"Nice," he commented. "This is more like it."

I wished he'd get on with it; I could do without the art appreciation.

We watched while he laid it face down on the cloth and set to work as he had done before. I wished I could get up and walk about. Anything to relieve the tension inside me. But I couldn't take my eyes off the old man's hands. Rekha was leaning forward, intent. Even Rumbelow and the sergeant had moved a step nearer the table. I supposed the room was air-conditioned but suddenly it seemed close, airless.

It didn't take long, then Hutchinson took the stretchers out of the frame and leaned forward to look more closely at the back of the canvas.

"There's two pictures 'ere," he announced.

I was conscious of my heart beating. He turned the stretchers so that we could see. Protruding from beneath the edge of the canvas where it was tacked down was another. I heard Perring blow through his teeth in a half-whistle.

"Looks like you were right," he observed, looking across at me.

Rumbelow said nothing.

We watched Hutchinson remove the tacks, lift off the portrait and lay it carefully on one side, then a sheet of thin plastic. Beneath it was a painting of a group in eighteenth-century dress, the men in breeches and buckled shoes, the women in hoops and panniers. The colours glowed but the expressions of the two central figures, a man and a woman, were so bored they were almost caricatures.

"*Marriage à la Mode,*" Rekha murmured.

"All right," Rumbelow said. He didn't sound too displeased.

The tension was easing out of me and I wondered why I

felt so little sense of triumph. Only a sudden almost over-
whelming weariness.

"It's a second version of one of the series; Hogarth
painted it for a friend," I said. Bill Mackay had told me that
on the phone; I supposed his reporter had got it from
Canadoc Glenn.

"But why smuggle it out like that?" Perring wanted to
know. "They could've packed it in a case with other stuff
without all this fuss."

"This was safer. If anyone did open the case they'd find a
picture with all the proper documentation and a genuine
export licence. If Fucillo kept getting crates of all sorts of
goods delivered to his gallery, people might have started
asking questions. And this way they didn't have to bring in
outsiders."

"But why the copy?"

"Bridgeman must have reckoned I'd go back to the shed
to have a look so he made sure there'd be something there
for me to find. He probably guessed Mrs. Graham would
tell me about his buying the portrait today so he got his wife
to paint a copy in acrylics. They dry very quickly and he
smudged dirt on it to make it look old. She's copied pictures before—they've at least one in their drawing-room—
and I don't suppose she asked why he wanted it. I'd told
him I knew next to nothing about paintings and he counted
on its being good enough to fool me."

"Only it wasn't," Rekha said quietly.

"It just didn't look right," I told her.

"It was clever," Rumbelow admitted. "All right, Mr.
Fordham, we'll have to take a statement from you now. And
you too, please, madam."

The statements took some time and he came back into
the room as we were signing them. We said good night and
went out into the corridor.

"Oh no!" I muttered.

"What is it?" Rekha enquired.

I had seen the truth that I should have seen before. It had come suddenly when I wasn't thinking about it any longer, perhaps because my brain was so tired. I knew now who was the brains behind the racket.

"Nothing," I said. "I must have another word with Rumbelow; it won't take a minute."

There was something I wanted to tell him I didn't want her to hear.

He looked round as I came in again and shut the door behind me.

"Yes, Mr. Fordham?" Even now his tone was cold and remote.

I explained.

"What are you going to do about them?" I finished.

He frowned. "You'll have to leave that to us."

I told him what was on my mind. He didn't like it but in the end he agreed.

SIXTEEN

Dawn was streaking the sky over the City. Beside me Rekha stifled a yawn. For the last few hours I had nearly forgotten the barrier between us and it had almost seemed she had too; now we were alone I was conscious of it again.

"I'm sorry I dragged you into that," I told her. Even to me it sounded stiff and absurdly formal.

"It doesn't matter." Her tone suggested she was too tired to care, and from the way she got into the Cortina her leg still hurt. "What are you going to do now?"

"Take you home, then go back to bed."

I had forgotten something else—we were going to start the harvest this morning. With luck I might get two or three hours' sleep first.

Already the streets were coming to life. I had always liked this time of the day, before most people were about, when driving along even the most mundane streets was a minor adventure.

"You could sleep at the flat," Rekha said. Her tone was matter-of-fact; she didn't want me to stay but felt she should make the offer. In the morning we would both be embarrassed. But I nearly accepted.

"I have to get back," I told her. "We're starting combining today. Thank you all the same."

She didn't press me and perversely I wished she had. Even though I would still have said no.

We drove up the hill and turned into her road. There

were no signs of life here; workaday traffic didn't pass Corhampton Court.

"I'll come up with you," I told her.

"It isn't necessary."

"Probably not," I agreed. "But I'll feel better if I do." It was unlikely any of Bridgeman's crowd would be there but I wasn't prepared to chance her going up alone.

We climbed the stairs. The whole block was quiet as a tomb. On the landing I told her, "You wait here. If I shout, run for it. Try to get to a phone and ring Rumbelow."

"Clive?" she said.

"Yes?"

She hesitated. "Nothing."

I took her key, watched her retreat to the bend in the stairs and opened the door. Silence inside too. The living-room door was open a few inches as we had left it. I tiptoed across the hall and listened. The only sound was the ticking of the clock on the sideboard. I pushed the door open hard and watched it bounce back off the stop. Counted to ten and switched on the light. The room was deserted. I went through to the kitchen, then both bedrooms and the bathroom. There was no-one in any of them.

Rekha was waiting on the landing.

"It's all right," I told her.

She nodded and led the way back to the living-room.

"I suppose it's no use my saying I'm sorry," I said.

"Are you, Clive?"

"Yes, really." I paused, wondering how to ask her, then came straight out with it. "Shall I see you again?"

"I don't know. I don't want to be hurt any more." She was avoiding my eyes.

"I'd better go," I said.

"Yes. Thank you for coming up. You're going to have a short night, aren't you?"

I wondered what she would say if I tried to kiss her and decided not to risk it.

She came to the flat door with me. "I'm glad it's all over," she said.

I knew she meant the business of the pictures and Bridgeman. So was I.

When she said good night there was a wistful note in her voice. Or perhaps I imagined it.

Heavy lorries rumbled along the M1, heading for the Midlands and the North; early loads of fruit and vegetables from Covent Garden. Not many cars. By the time I turned on to the track to my house it was almost light. I found it hard to believe it was only a week since Graham crashed, so much had happened since then, some good, most of it bad. I wondered if my life would ever be quite the same again. Maybe in a few months, when the trial was over, it would all seem like a dream.

It was too much trouble to put the car away in the barn; all I wanted was to fall into bed. I left it in the yard, fished my key out of my pocket and unlocked the back door, reaching for the light switch. I knew the truth now. So did Rumbelow. In a few hours it would all be over.

Two men were standing by the table. One was Bridgeman. He was wearing a sweater and light trousers and apart from the dark shadow of stubble round his jaw looked as sleek as ever. Fucillo was near the living-room door. It occurred to me that in spite of his bulk there was something almost reptilian about him. I didn't like the look in his eyes. Still less did I like the gun he was holding, the same small black pistol he had had at the gallery. And again it was pointing straight at my heart.

Oh God! I thought.

"Shut the door and sit down," Bridgeman told me harshly.

I stayed where I was; they wouldn't shoot me for that. They were here because they wanted to know what I had done with the pictures and a dead man couldn't tell them. I wished I had waited to replace the hardboard behind Bridgeman's bench, then they might not have known so soon I had taken the original Leclerc and the Hogarth. But I had been in too much of a hurry to get away.

There was a thump in the room over the kitchen; one of the spare bedrooms. Footsteps crossed the floor. I guessed Foskett and his mate Andrews were up there searching.

"How did you get in this time?" I asked.

"The front door."

At this rate soon I wouldn't have any woodwork left. "I'll see about getting it done in the morning," I said.

"I wouldn't count on it." Bridgeman's meaning was only too clear.

I hadn't reckoned on their getting here for another couple of hours. The fact that they were about so early suggested something was about to happen. Had they planned to move the pictures today? Now the Hogarth was safely concealed, or they believed it was, it could be taken to the gallery to await the licence and other documents for sending it to Fucillo in New York.

"What have you come for?" I demanded.

This time Bridgeman didn't answer; he just went on staring at me with his cold, heavily lidded eyes. Then he sat down at the table and rested his hands on it. They were white and fleshy.

A minute ticked by. Two. I guessed they were trying to unnerve me, softening me up for whatever was to come. If so they were succeeding.

The noises overhead had stopped and I heard footsteps

coming down the stairs. They crossed the hall, the door opened and Foskett came in followed by Andrews. I hadn't seen him clearly at Rekha's flat—there hadn't been time before the rough-and-tumble started—and I didn't care for what I saw now. He was about twenty-five with a low forehead and hardly any neck, so that his head seemed to rest almost on his shoulders. His eyes were too close together under heavy black brows that met over the bridge of his nose. A mean-looking thug.

"They're not there," Foskett reported. "We've turned the whole place over." He gave me a look that was half triumph, half hate. He was glad to see me there. Apart from interfering in their activities, I had kneed him painfully twice at the flat and he believed I had taken his place with Stephanie. A man like Foskett could hate for a lot less than that.

"What have you done with them?" Bridgeman demanded, looking at me. His voice was flat, unemotional.

"Done with what?" I asked.

"Don't be a fool. Where are the pictures you stole from my shed tonight?"

"What are you talking about? Why should I steal any pictures from you?"

"Where have you been?" Fucillo demanded. It was the first time he had spoken.

"To London, to see a friend."

"The Graham woman," Foskett said.

"All right," I agreed, "I went to see Mrs. Graham. What about it?"

"He's lying," Bridgeman said flatly.

"You can ring her in the morning and ask her if you don't believe me," I told him. Too late I realised I might be putting Rekha in danger. But Rumbelow would have acted by then.

Bridgeman still didn't believe me. "You came to my house and stole two paintings. You broke into my shed to get them; they're valuable and I want them back. Let me have them and we won't say anything about your breaking in."

"I don't know anything about your paintings. How the hell should I?"

"Don't play games, Fordham. Where are they?"

"I haven't got them. Your two goons there told you that. And I didn't take them to Mrs. Graham." I hope that sounded more convincing to them than it did to me.

Foskett walked over and hit me across the face with the back of his hand. Hard. Instinctively I took a step forward and started to swing a punch at his jaw. Andrews grabbed me from behind and pulled me back, gripping my arms. I tried to shrug him off but it was like wrestling with an octopus.

Foskett grinned and hit me again, this time a full-blooded punch in the pit of my stomach that sent the breath tearing out of my lungs. I gasped.

"That's enough," Bridgeman told him sharply.

The breath came back painfully. I wondered if Bridgeman suspected what I had done with the pictures and was tempted to tell him just to see the effect. But once they knew I had been to the police my life expectancy would be about five minutes. I would be no more use to them and they would kill me from anger or a desire for revenge. Revenge was probably one of Fucillo's strongest emotions. They had already been concerned in Williamson's murder and you could only serve "life" once.

It wasn't a comforting thought but they were going to kill me anyway; I had no illusions about that. It was merely a matter of time. And time was something I hadn't got. All the same, I had no intention of making things easy for them. If they were so anxious to know where the paintings were, the longer it took them to find out the better. At least while there was life there was hope. Not much. Practically none, in fact, but even that was better than none at all.

I looked at Foskett. "How are you making out with Stephanie, Foskett? Had any luck there lately?"

Bridgeman turned his head that way. His eyes narrowed.

"Did you know he's been having a bit on the side with her?" I asked him.

"Shut your bloody mouth!" Foskett roared. He made a swift, violent move towards me but Bridgeman stopped him.

"What do you mean?" he demanded harshly.

"You mean you don't know? At your party on Saturday I caught him sneaking up to her room while you were talking to people outside. Why do you think he was so furious when I brought her home the other evening? He thought I'd been taking his place and he was jealous. Maybe he reckoned you wouldn't dare do anything about it because he knew too much."

"You bloody—" Foskett began. He looked capable of strangling me on the spot. But he was afraid of Bridgeman.

"Is it true?" Bridgeman was staring at him and his tone cut like a whip.

"No." The manager was starting to bluster. Perhaps he knew Stephanie would betray him if her father taxed her with the truth. Very likely she would put the blame on him too, say he had forced himself on her. "He's making it up. He's the one who—"

Bridgeman stood up. I realised I had never seen him really angry before. And where Foskett was all temper and bluster, he was ice-cold. He might be several inches the shorter and, even now, slightly pompous, but there was nothing ridiculous about him. He reached out, grasped

Foskett's collar and shook him like a dog. Then he struck him a blow across his face that sent him reeling.

"Cut it out, both of you," Fucillo told them curtly.

But Bridgeman wasn't listening. "If you've been messing around with Stephanie I'll make you wish you'd never been born," he grated. His eyes were hot with rage.

"She as good as admitted it when I brought her home last night," I reminded him. "You heard her."

Even then he hadn't faced the truth. Now he could no longer avoid it.

For several seconds they stood there, staring at each other like two animals. Then Fucillo stepped between them and pushed them apart. For a second his gun was no longer pointing at me. I lunged forward, pulling Andrews with me. The sudden movement caught him off balance and his grip on my arms relaxed. Perhaps he had been too interested in what was happening to concentrate on restraining me. I grabbed for the American's wrist. My outstretched fingers touched it. Then a hand like a vice clamped round my arm and dragged me back. Andrews had regained his balance more quickly than I had anticipated.

"Don't be a fool, Clive," Eunice Bridgeman said coolly.

I had been half expecting her but still I hadn't heard her come in. I turned. She was standing just inside the door wearing the shirt and trousers she had worn on Monday evening when she drove down to Somerset and shot Williamson. The same flat driving shoes, scuffed round the heels. I had noticed them when she came in that evening after I took Stephanie home and been surprised she had worn such old clothes even to visit a friend. Other times when I had seen her she had been smartly dressed.

Stephanie had told me her step-mother had gone somewhere. When we got to the house Bridgeman and Foskett were both there while Fucillo and Andrews had given Stephanie a lift to the village less than an hour before. There was no car outside the house when we drove up. Eunice came in and five minutes later when I left the Jaguar was there, its engine still hot and its bodywork splashed with reddish mud. It had had to be her or Peter and I couldn't believe it was him.

"Surprised to see me?" There was nothing of the homely housewife now. The quiet strength I had seen before had become a cold ruthlessness.

"No."

I saw the flicker of anger cross her face; she had wanted me to be surprised. But she was in charge, there was no doubt about that.

"Tie him to that chair," she said.

"Like hell you do!" I retorted.

This was the crunch. I had been playing for time and now it had run out.

Foskett pulled out one of the kitchen chairs from under the table, brought it round behind me and shoved it hard against the back of my legs. Andrews forced me down on to it. He held me while Foskett lashed my wrists together, pulling the cord so tight it bit deep into my flesh. Then he bound my ankles and tied them to the rail of the chair. All the time he grinned.

"Now where are the pictures?" Eunice demanded.

"I don't know anything about them."

She went through to the old scullery. I could hear her rooting about out there and wondered what she was doing. Whatever it was, I was pretty sure I wouldn't like it.

After a minute or two she returned carrying an old poker. I waited, tense, for the blow. But it didn't come. Instead she walked round behind me. I felt the cold metal against my wrists. They were tied so tightly there was hardly room for a piece of paper between them but she forced the poker in somehow.

"All right, Lew," she said.

She walked across to the table and he took her place at my back. For a second I didn't understand, then he twisted the poker viciously. The cords cut deeper into my wrists.

"Why don't you make it easier for yourself?" he enquired almost amiably.

And get shot straightaway? I thought. I reckoned I could hang on a bit longer yet.

For what?

I didn't know.

Fucillo gave the poker another turn. Pain shot up my arms.

"We'll give him a few minutes to think about it," Eunice said.

She sat down near her husband, the others remained where they were. The seconds ticked by on the grandfather clock in the living-room and every minute seemed like an hour. None of them spoke. It was strange, my hands felt dead and on fire at the same time. Something to do with the circulation. Only there wasn't any. I could feel the sweat on my forehead and tried to force myself to think of something else. Anything but the agonising pain of my hands and arms.

I had suggested to Rumbelow that his men come here in another hour or so. When they arrived I would ring Eunice and tell her I had the paintings. That was bound to bring one of them over, possibly all three of them; Foskett and Andrews didn't count. When they got here, Rumbelow's men would hear enough to arrest them. It wasn't very subtle but it was so simple I reckoned it would work.

He hadn't bothered to hide his disapproval but he knew he hadn't much in the way of firm evidence and in the end he had gone along with it. Neither of us had foreseen Bridgeman's discovering the damage to the shed door before seven o'clock at the earliest. Now they would arrive too late. They would find nothing here or at Langley Farm. Even the shed door would have been repaired, Eunice wouldn't overlook that.

And I would be dead.

Rekha was in bed, probably asleep. How distressed would she be? When I had left her tonight I had believed there was a chance we could put the last two days behind us. Now I would never know.

Foskett was staring at me, looking as if he would boil over if he didn't get rid of some of the anger and tension inside him. Suddenly he walked over and struck me across the mouth. I felt my lip split and tasted blood.

"Stop that!" Eunice told him sharply.

I guessed she wanted me to have nothing to concentrate on but the cord cutting into my wrists and the increasing pain of my hands. Wondering what was going to happen to me next. Foskett was giving me something else to think about.

"Let's get on with it," Bridgeman said impatiently. "I want those bloody pictures."

Eunice gave Fucillo a slight nod. The poker twisted the cord again cruelly. This time I couldn't suppress a grunt of pain.

"Where are they?" he grated.

My hands were like lumps of raw meat, swollen and dead. How long did it take for gangrene to set in? I had no idea.

I asked myself what difference it made what happened, I couldn't stall them until Rumbelow's men arrived. All I wanted was for the torture to stop. I remembered when I had bad appendicitis as a boy not caring about anything but an end to the appalling pain. Why not tell them? Nobody would suffer but me.

"The police have got them," I mumbled. My broken lip was swelling.

"You're lying," Bridgeman told me.

Why couldn't they believe me now I was telling the truth? Whatever I said was a lie.

"That's where I went." My head was swimming. "Scotland Yard. They've got them all."

Now they knew. They would kill me but that would be that, I wouldn't have to worry any more.

"I guess he's telling the truth now," Fucillo said.

"I don't believe him." Some of Bridgeman's old chilly calm had returned. "I think he took them to the Graham woman."

"Why should he?" Eunice wasn't sure yet. She stood staring at me, her face as expressionless as a mask.

"If 'e's bin to the police they'll know ev'rythink," Andrews put in. He had a London accent and he sounded scared. "They'll come 'ere."

"Shut up," Bridgeman told him harshly.

"I'm going."

"Stay where you are," Eunice ordered.

"Not bloody likely. You killed the old man, they're not doing me for that."

He started towards the door. Fucillo was still behind me and I didn't see his right hand go to his pocket. The report close to my head nearly deafened me.

I read somewhere once that if you aren't used to handling guns it's easier to miss someone standing a few feet away than it is to hit them. And if he's on edge, even an experienced marksman will miss. The odds are you'll put a bullet in a wall or the floor. Fucillo's shot struck Andrews just below his left shoulder-blade. He staggered slightly as if someone had pushed him, then he slumped against the wall and slid down it to the floor. Fucillo fired again. The inert form twitched horribly and was still.

Nobody spoke. Foskett looked shaken but neither Eunice nor her husband showed any emotion. There was a sickening acrid smell in the room.

Next time it would be me, I thought. Would I hear the shot? I shivered uncontrollably against the ropes.

"Untie his legs," Eunice said, looking at me.

Foskett obeyed.

"Take Andrews outside, then come back for him." She turned to me. "We're going to dump you both in your corn store. There's a load of barley outside; it'll be a long time before anybody finds you under that."

I felt cold right deep down in my stomach. Imagined the corn cascading on top of me. Tons of it. But maybe Rumbelow would start a search before then.

Foskett had to pull Andrews away from the door to open it. I watched him pick up the body, sling it over his shoulder and carry it outside. Daylight streamed in at the open window. It was later than I thought. But still not late enough.

We waited in silence and after a minute or so Foskett returned.

"Okay," Fucillo told me. "On your feet."

I hardly heard him. Now it had come to it I could scarcely accept this was happening to me.

"You've asked for it."

He pulled the poker, jerking my arms upwards into the small of my back. The pain was excruciating.

"Now will you?" he demanded.

I stood up. Nearly fell; my legs felt like jelly. Fucillo gave me a push and I staggered. Eunice was watching me. No hope there, her eyes were as cold as marbles. I walked unsteadily to the door.

So this was it. I knew now what a condemned man felt like on his way to execution. It was knowledge I could have done without.

We went out in single file, Eunice bringing up the rear. Two cars were coming up the lane from the main road; they might as well have been a hundred miles away.

"Over there," Fucillo told me, pushing me towards the end barn.

I obeyed, walking as slowly as I could.

"Hurry it up," Bridgeman said impatiently.

A part of my mind registered that the first car was almost level with the end of the track. But it was being driven fast. At that speed, even if he looked this way, the driver wouldn't notice anything wrong.

Then everything seemed to start happening at once. Tyres screaming, the car turned in at the gate and headed straight for us, the second one only just behind it.

"The police!" Foskett exclaimed.

The cars were bumping along the track. When the leading one was only thirty or forty yards away Fucillo fired. The explosion rocked me. I heard a clang as the bullet hit metal and threw myself backwards, cannoning into him. The impact sent him reeling and when he fired again the shot went wide.

The cars stopped and men poured out. I saw Bridgeman running towards the barn where I kept my car; he must have put his there out of sight. Foskett had stopped halfway across the yard. For a moment he stood there staring at the men running towards us, then he too turned and fled. Eunice hadn't moved.

"Put your gun down and raise your hands," a man shouted.

For answer Fucillo fired again. One of the policemen

stumbled and fell. I rolled over and saw them fanning out
on both sides of the cars. One of them raised both hands
straight in front of him, taking aim. He fired a fraction of a
second before the American and Fucillo pitched forward,
clutching his leg. The gun fell from his hand and clattered
away across the concrete.

For a moment it was very quiet. Eunice was looking down
at Fucillo. Then Rumbelow walked over to where I was
lying. I hadn't the strength to get up and, anyway, I
couldn't use my hands.

"You all right?" he enquired.

I nodded. "You're early."

"Just as well from the look of it." He reached down to
help me to my feet and saw the poker jammed between my
wrists. "Hell!"

Taking out a knife, he sawed through the cord. For two or
three seconds the relief was exquisite. Then feeling started
coming back into my hands and I had to stop myself from
screaming. He put a hand on my arm to support me.

"Bridgeman's in the second barn there," I told him. "I
don't think he's got a gun but I'm not sure. And there's one
of them in the corn store. Dead. Fucillo shot him."

The American was still lying on the ground, swearing.
Rumbelow told one of his men to help me into the house
and went to have a look at him. The policeman was young
and looked tough but he treated me as if I were a delicate
old lady.

"Are you going to be all right?" he asked when he had
seen me seated more or less comfortably in one of the easy
chairs.

I nodded. Talking was too much effort.

"We'd better get a doctor to have a look at you. Do you
know his number?"

I didn't; I hadn't seen a doctor professionally since I broke my right leg four years ago. Except Ravi the other night.

"His name's Vernon," I said.

The policeman found his number in the directory and dialled it. I heard him ask if the doctor could come over right away and wondered what the urgency was about, I wasn't going to die. Not yet, anyway. And I certainly wasn't going to run away.

"He's coming," he said, putting down the phone. "If you're okay I'd better get back outside."

Left alone, I was almost overcome by a feeling of lassitude. I started shivering uncontrollably and went on, as if I had an ague. It was ridiculous, I told myself: I should have been on top of the world. I was alive; that in itself was some sort of miracle.

Rumbelow came in to tell me they had rounded up Bridgeman and Foskett. Bridgeman had been trying to start his car but in his haste he had stalled the engine twice. I thought of Eunice standing calmly, waiting, when she knew there was no point any longer in trying to escape. I had been right about that at least. When it came to the crunch Bridgeman was a mean, little man while she retained a sort of dignity, tarnished though it was. Foskett had been caught fleeing towards his house. He would keep his gun there as well as his car.

"Was there anyone else involved, do you know?" I asked Rumbelow. "Apart from the girl at the gallery?"

I was still worrying about Peter.

"No."

Thank God.

We talked for a few minutes, then the doctor arrived and Rumbelow left us. Doctor Vernon was about forty and tall.

He examined me with a thoroughness I thought a bit over-
done, considering I was all right apart from some nasty
weals on my wrists. When I took my shirt off and he saw the
bruises on my side he wanted to know where I had got
them.

"The same way," I answered. I wasn't sure how much he
knew and guessed it wasn't much.

He smiled ironically. "Farming seems to be changing."

"It is," I agreed.

He told me that as far as he could see I hadn't suffered
any serious damage and should be as good as new in a few
days. Then he put dressings on my wrists, gave me a couple
of pills and advised me to go to bed.

I took his advice but not his pills; I was pretty sure I
wouldn't need them to help me sleep.

I was right.

When I woke there was somebody else in the room. I
turned my head, expecting to see a policeman or, possibly,
Elizabeth. It was neither of them.

"Rekha!" I exclaimed.

She came round to the side of the bed. "Hallo, Clive."

"What are you doing here?"

She smiled. "Mr. Rumbelow said you might need looking
after."

"Rumbelow?"

"He rang me."

That was as big a surprise as her being here. I wondered
how much he had told her.

"How do you feel?" she asked.

"Better now you're here." It was true, I felt light-headed.

She leaned forward and kissed me as she had done before, on the mouth gently. Then not as she had done before. I heard her sigh but it didn't sound like a sigh of

regret. I put my arms round her but with the bandages on my wrists I could hardly feel her.

"How long can you stay?" I asked her.

"That's up to you," she answered. Then she kissed me again.

About the Author

IAN STUART is a successful writer living in England. He is the author of twelve previous mystery novels, including *A Growing Concern* and *The Garb of Truth* published by the Crime Club.